The Swines

Anecdotes Of A Piggly Family

THE SWINES

ANECDOTES OF A PIGGLY FAMILY

A Novel

H. M. So

"When you stop and think about what you are, it's like trying to catch a flowing stream."

CONTENTS

The Swines

ANECDOTES OF A PIGGLY FAMILY

THE SWINES

1

MEET THE SWINES

"If you need a dictionary, you're trying too hard."

I come from a family of pigs. My mom is a British Lop, of which she is quite proud. Though only of piggly stock, she's British through and through with the same concomitant air of imperial pride known only among the English. Her great-great-great-great-grandmother was once the main course for the queen herself. To this day her side of the family in Cornwall speak of it with intumescent pride and hoity-toity superiority. The local British papers reported the pork was the finest to be ever served the royal family. "Soft, moist and delicious white and dark meat," it said. "And glazed with a fusion of honey, brown sugar, cumin, basil, and secret royal herbs." Personally, I don't care much for British royalty. I just wish my mom showered and cleaned the house like the rest of the hoi polloi.

"Do you think I smell funny?" she sometimes asks.

It's hard to tell your mom that she smells like a *pig* and not in a good way.

"Of course I smell like a pig! I am a pig!" she declares.

Hearts are frangible.

My father is a warthog, the pedigree, I'm not quite sure. I think his family originally comes from the sweltering plains of the African savannas. I don't think he knows either or really cares. He's a bit rough around the edges. He's a boar through and through, and boorish from hoof to tusk, my mom says, when she's not in the nicest mood. He can be a philistine.

His mornings start with guttural noises and proceeds through the day with various kinds of somatic disturbances no child should learn about until he gets married. He grunts in the hallway just outside my room, coughs up phlegm, and drools like a busted faucet. And when he's not quite the center of attention he thinks he ought to be, he howls like a batshoot crazy hog. When I complain about the noise, Mom always comes to his support. She's his number one excuse attorney.

"He's not yelling. He's just loud," she asserts in his defense. "That's his normal voice. He's always a few decibels too high. *You know that.*"

My parents get into arguments sometimes about some silly thing or another. They're never too bad but voices are raised, snorts turn to hollering, and neighbors sometimes peek through the windows. My hirsute father has tusks that could split open an elephant (he claims) but his booms are generally louder than his bite. He says his grandfather once impaled a lion. My mom's snout is pretty formidable as well. You don't want her breathing down your neck. The viscous liquid that dribbles from her nostrils can suffocate a large fish.

Me? I'm Sam. And I'm twelve. I started middle school and I'm a straight A student. Or at least I used to be. Middle school is a new adventure and I'm not quite sure how I'll do. I've heard anecdotes of kids going from hero to sub-zero because they couldn't handle teachers and prepubescent peer pressure. I have a few friends, but girls give me the heebie-jeebies. My mom and dad also don't make the best first impressions at PTA and parent-to-parent back slapping shindigs. My friends tell me that I'm so different from my parents. But I'm not adopted. Really. My family is swine but I'm perfectly normal.

* * *

My favorite subjects are math, history, and English. I think math is important because it impels the mind to the logical. "There are no wishy washy, opinionated answers to math problems," Mr. McCoy, my teacher, says. You're either right or wrong and he'll be the final arbiter of that, he proclaims.

History, on the other hand, is arguably a lot more subjective. Dates may be factual but exactly what happened on that day is another story. According to Mr. Johnson, "history is the opinion of historians, professors, and nerds who spend a lot of time at the library." But in the end, it's just a point of view. Or as Napoleon Bonaparte once said, "history is full of lies people agree on to believe."

Of course, history isn't always so dubious. According to the Eastern sage, Confucius, the best way to "determine the future is to learn from the past." But which lessons are we meant to learn? If only we were smart enough to know. Or is the past meant to be retold differently every time in service of the present? That seems so cynical!

Maybe English, like all languages, is a bridge between make believe and truth. It helps communicate what we think and feel. It may be true or not true in the opinion of some, but if you're honest with yourself, then it's at least true for you at this moment. Unfortunately, my English teacher is a shrew named Ms. Fearstein and everything I say seems to be untrue for her. I once brought her an apple and she hit me on the head with it.

"What did you do that for?" I cried.

"Sorry, kiddo. I thought it was a tennis ball," she answered without remorse. "Now, take a seat before I serve you another one."

On the classroom wall there are posters of Shakespeare's famous plays. The English poet wrote about comedy, tragedy and tragicomedy.

I think she hates me.

* * *

My best friends are Danny and Scott. We're almost two months into the new school year and except for assault and battery by the not-to-be-named English teacher, things are going pretty well. It's nice to have friends in a sea of anxious prepubescent teens. A kid could get swallowed up in the ocean.

I've known Danny since the second grade. And Scott was the new boy in school in the fourth. He lives in a white house on the other side of town. His Dad is a dentist. Danny lives down the street in a beige condominium. His father works for a delivery company. According to kid years, we've been friends a long time. Of course, to adults, it's just a handful of seasons. A blip in the calendar. My mom has underpants older than all of our ages combined.

I hope middle school will be fun. Maybe there's a naive anticipation for something that's unrealistic. But so far, so good. We have our own personal lockers, and change classes after each period. Kids crowd into the halls like morning subway commuters except there are no trains and we have nowhere to go except down the hall. From a vertical distance we must resemble lost ants trudging back and forth.

* * *

My parents are blue collar folks who speak plainly. Dad says, if you need a dictionary, you're trying too hard. My mom likes literature in theory, but she says it makes her drowsy. She thinks it might be allergies.

According to his calculations, Dad says we're middle class. That means our family makes an yearly income that's about average, although I'm guessing average, like history, can be very subjective while pretending to convey a precision closer to math. My friend, Scott, says his family is average, but they live in a large six bedroom house with a pool, own four motorcycles, a boat, three cars, and travel to Europe every summer. We have one car and vacation by driving endlessly on barren, dirt roads. Extended arms out open windows imitating the flight of wings count as entertainment.

My dad used to be a plumber and ran his own small business. He's semi-retired now and gets work occasionally from previous customers. He charges half rate and receives payments in cash. My dad doesn't believe in cryptocurrencies or credit cards. He believes in precious metals, cold green cash, and grain storage silos. We have a mini grain silo in the backyard next to the buried gold bars and dried meats.

Mom is retired, too, but keeps herself busy in the garden. She used to be a florist and had a small shop she rented from Mr. Sosa, an old man originally from Brazil. "We love our barbecue in Brazil," he used to say, licking his lips and firmly but gently pulling her thick hands toward his mouth. He said his favorite Brazilian BBQ was Costela de Porco Assada. My mother thought he was a little too friendly and strange, but he was a nice man and gave her a good deal on the rent until he passed away. When the new owner brought it up to market rates, she retired.

My dad bought our three bedroom house in Suidae Valley about eleven years ago when I was a baby. Suidae Valley had a nice ring to it, Mom said, and they decided to make their home here. It's a medium sized town somewhere in the middle of California between Porterville and Salinas. We have cows, horses, and other livestock in the area. But we might be the only pigs. Dad added an extra room downstairs a few years ago to make into a play pen for Mom. It's literally a pig pen now.

We fit right in with everyone here. *Suids* are nice, friendly people. The town mascot is a *Chester White,* but Mom says *Lops* are more tender cuts of meat and better mannered.

Sometimes they ask us where we're from. Mom proudly tells them she's from Cornwall, England. Dad grunts and says his ancestors fought in the Civil War—for the right side. I assume he means the Union? I don't know if that's true but it's quite a pedigree for a sub-Saharan wild African boar. I think we have relatives back in Texas.

Dad moved out to California when he was younger and dreamed of settling the West. He thought Los Angeles was too show business and San Francisco was overrun with vegan hippies. So he chose a quiet town in between where he could avoid the paparazzi and enjoy red, juicy steak. Mom says she wouldn't mind being a movie star or joining a commune. She thinks she has a face for television and the perfect body for manual labor. She claims she can outwork a horse. Dad's not sure if she can work harder than a horse, but she can eat as much.

* * *

I haven't decided what I want to be when I grow up. When you're a kid, everything seems possible. I took a month of piano lessons and people said I was a musician. I wrote a short story in the sixth grade that won a second place blue ribbon for best fiction and I was celebrated as an up and coming writer by the contest organizers. After a month of Spanish lessons the teacher said we were bilingual. But all I could say was "si," "que?" and "como te llamas?" It seems a kid could qualify to be almost anything with a little effort.

But adulthood is different. You can't pass yourself off as a pianist because you play a few bars of chopsticks. Genuine expertise requires a lot of time and skill, which means ten thousand hours of practice according to conventional wisdom. Ten thousand hours of practice is more than a year without sleep and food or ten years practicing three hours a day. My dad says it took him many years to go from apprentice to master plumber. He says it's a lot harder than it looks. It's not just throwing Liquid Draymo down pipes and collecting forty bucks. Sometimes you have to stick your head under the sink and get water splashed on your face. That means dedication and commitment to a craft. I'm just not sure what that is yet. A year is a long time for a kid to go without sleep and food.

Mr. McCoy thinks I have a binary future in mathematics. It could go positively. Or negatively. The unknown variable is whether I can ace next week's algebra exam on polynomial functions. Mr. Johnson says my preternatural talent for dates, narrative, and revisionist interpretation bends the arc of history toward justice. Or maybe fiction. My answers to yesterday's pop quiz on Columbus are sure to offend everyone on all sides of the historical debate. But Ms. Fearstein says I should give up now. No point in the pretension that I have any future at all. She says that as a student, I'm not half bad, but that doesn't mean the other half is any good.

I think a kid should be allowed to be a kid without so many adult hands trying to shape it. We're flesh, blood, and sticky sweat, after all, not modeling clay. Except, there's an interregnum between childhood and adulthood that can really throw things for a loop if it goes off the rails, Mom says. I'm entering that phase now and have to be careful. The age between twelve and twenty-one are the most unpredictable and treacherous. But Dad says I should do what I want. Have fun! Let the devil take tomorrow.

2

VEGETABLE ASSIGNMENT

*"The idea of vegetables agitated him
like sticky rice in his pants."*

Friday morning began with the usual early raucous of sounds, noises, grunts, and somatic explosions. Coughs and the cacophony of phlegm from Dad and a loud random *yaaawwwaaahhhh!* just because.

From the kitchen emerged the rackety sounds of clacking dishes, utensils, pots *(bang!)*, and mixers *(vroooom!)*. Though she seemed extremely busy, what Mom was exactly doing, no one really knew for sure.

Then there was the dissonant reminder from the alarm

clock that signaled the conclusion of my dreams and the commencement of another school day. While not quite a nightmare and gulag for children, school isn't something one chooses to get up for on a cold morning day in lieu of a warm, soft bed, especially in the middle of something important. No one likes being interrupted during a fierce battle with zombies in the grisly bosom of the Apocalypse. "I'll be back tonight after school and homework!" I promise the undead. I don't want to miss the end of the world.

I went to the bathroom, brushed my teeth, and washed my face. I put on old pants I hadn't worn yesterday and then noticed crumpled paper in my back pocket. I opened it up: SCHOOL ASSIGNMENT — VEGETABLES. I had forgotten. I was supposed to give it to Mom.

We're learning about vegetables at school but I didn't think my parents would be too keen on it. It doesn't resemble even remotely what we eat +at home, which are mostly slaughtered bovine carcasses and poultry. And starches like potatoes and rice.

Mom was a *binivore.* Strictly starches and meats. Dad, on the other hand, was somewhat more selective with his diet: meats only. Only meats. Just meats. Red blooded meats. Nothing but meats. If it wasn't slain, it's not edible, was his credo. Of course, pigs are supposed to eat everything, but we weren't ordinary pigs.

"What's all this about vegetables?!" Dad bellowed.

He was in a particularly foul mood today and the idea of vegetables agitated him like sticky rice in his pants. He did not approve and his booming orifice was ejecting slobber rockets like B-52 bombers.

"Is this America or some third world country that we have to eat barks and leaves?!" he growled, drooling and driveling, forcing me to take cover on the other side of the room. It was like napalm in the morning except the smell was worse.

"Don't mind Dad," Mom said. "He hasn't been able to poop in seventeen days. He's very backed up. I love veggies. Plantains, sweet potatoes and raviolis . . ."

"That's all commie and hippie food!" Dad hollered with more spittles of yellow phlegm. "And don't talk about my poop! That's personal."

"No, Mom. Potatoes aren't really vegetables," I tried to explain. I was like a desperate Vietnamese villager dodging aerial bombs. "That's a starch. And plantains and raviolis too."

"Starch is in the laundry room," Mom countered.

"No, no . . . a starch is a carbohydron," Dad thundered, dropping more saliva napalm. "It's what they ate during the war. Along with grass. There ain't no dang war! I'm a red-blooded hog. I need my proteins or I get allergies. *Acchhhooooooo!*"

Dad's allergies were acting up again along with a bevy of other ailments. Sometimes it gets so bad he calls the ambulance and goes to the hospital emergency room. He thinks it's some kind of first class medical service for VIPs because he doesn't have to queue for three hours like others in the waiting area.

"Well, here are some recipes from Sam's teacher, Ms. Jones. Maybe we should give it a try?" Mom said. "Let's see here . . . BROCCOLI. The instructions say to STEAM FOR TWENTY MINUTES. SALT. BUTTER. OLIVE OIL.

Sounds easy."

"Good grief! Ms. Jones can steam me some steak! You can steam whatever you want, including broccocrap." Dad was heaving now. Allergies, backed up plumbing, and unwelcome jungle vegetation were aggravating his emotional ecosystem.

"Sit on the toilet, dear. Maybe you'll feel better," Mom exhorted.

"I'm sitting on the sofa and watching the game!" Dad barked. "Poop will come out when it's ready to come out! If it takes another year, fine. It's not something I'm waiting around for. There's no hurry."

In between bites of my cereal, I wondered how I was going to escape my assignment and the rhetorical fusillade disturbing my own personal homeostasis. My emotional ecosystem was being tested, too, and it wouldn't take much to turn over a twelve-year-old's sensitive equilibrium.

"You're upset because you're constipated."

"Your nagging is constipating!"

Thankfully, the school bus had arrived and demanded my attention. The din of the blaring horn exceeded the ruckus of two squabbling middle-aged parents in the middle of matrimonial bliss. But the bus would mean being greeted to another kind of bedlam.

"Off to school!" I yelled, grabbing my backpack. I waved goodbye and ran out the house like an escaping refugee.

"Have a good day at school, Sam!" Mom shouted.

Inside the belly of the yellow tin can, I was ambushed by another melee. Crumpled papers showered down like miniature asteroids. Erasers bounced off the ceiling like ricocheting bullets. Wet projectiles resembling tiny cannon balls ejected from hollow tubes—formerly writing instruments—splattered on vinyl seats and startled fresh-faced victims.

And I was almost blinded by a paper plane that hit me straight between the eyes. *That should be illegal!* But I was too tired to join the mayhem. I was an escapee looking for asylum.

* * *

In health class, lessons on vegetables continued. Ms. Jones distributed graphs, fact sheets, and factoids. She entertained us with slide presentations and short video clips. Who knew that spinach originated in Persia and really did make you strong like Popeye? Well, almost.

"Scientific studies have shown that vegetables are essential for good health," Ms. Jones told the class. "Veggies contain important minerals, amino acids, micronutrients, and phytonutrients."

Our teacher was a slim thirty-something and adhered to a strictly vegan diet. She was popular with the male faculty at school but with women it was a more complicated relation. Maybe she was too skinny for her own good? Ms. Jones was an avid yoga practitioner and taught classes three times a week.

"Vegetables also help you avoid upset stomach, keep you regular, and are more gentle to the land and ecosystem," she said.

In fact, we learned that more people could be fed if we reduced our proportional intake of animal products and replaced it with plant based foods. Plants are good for ourselves and the environment.

"Fewer people in hospital beds mean more active people jogging in the park, exercising and doing yoga," she added.

Some of the biggest and most powerful animals in the world, like elephants, rhinos and gorillas, are also plant eaters. Notwithstanding what Dad says, energy and strength doesn't just come from steak. Carbs, essential for endurance, and proteins, the building blocks of muscles, are abundant in plant based foods.

* * *

When I came home from school, I was pooped. Our PE teacher made us run a whole mile. I was feeling bushed. Hungry. And despondent about my assignment. How will I make some vegetables? Dad was ideologically against it like a *#NeverVeggie* activist. And Mom hadn't a clue about anything green. She only knew white and brown, which she consumed like a pig. She stopped growing vertically a long time ago but her ankles resembled tree trunks.

When dinner was ready I rushed down like a famished beast propelling my homework papers flying into the air. I was probably the fastest runner in school. Some students and teachers speculated I had animal genes.

Dad sat at the front of the table with a big slab of steak.

"Ahooooo!" he yelled, signaling his readiness to devour it.

"Yikes! You scared the living daylights out of me," Mom complained, busily getting the rest of the food served. "How many times do I have to ask you not to yell?"

"I'm just expressing myself! I'm being a *natural* warthog. That's what we do! We *HOOOLLLLLLERRRRR!"*

I asked for vegetables but it was steak and rice for me, too, with a little side of garnish. Parsley growing wild in the garden seemed to be the best Mom could muster up.

Mom resigned herself to yesterday's leftovers. Some old chicken. And potatoes to clean it down. Someone had to finish off the old chow. Mom didn't like things going to waste. It would be very un-porcine of her.

"How's the assignment going?" Mom asked.

"Nowhere. DOA. Dead on arrival. I need to have some vegetables and learn what green stuff feels like in my mouth. You know, like food."

"There's some parsley on your plate. Chew on that."

"That's not enough, Mom! I need a plate of real, big vegetables. All kinds of vegetables."

"Rice is a vegetable."

"Not really. It's a starch."

"Are you sure? I always thought rice was a veggie."

"No . . ."

"For sure potatoes are veggies. Here, have some of mine."

"No, Mom! Potatoes are also a starch."

Nonstop talk about green food was giving Dad upset stomach. He was feeling queasy. He was up to his hairy ears with vegetables. It was fouling his mood and spoiling his medium rare, juicy steak dinner.

"Stop, stop!" he shouted. "Honey, why don't you take Sam to the supermarket and get him some of that broccolat. But if you get sick, Sam, it's not our fault!"

"Sick? Why would I get sick?" I demanded. "You can't get sick with vegetables. Ms. Jones says it's good for you."

"I've seen it happen! A friend of mine ate a bucket of coleslop and got sick. Don't think it can't happen. You don't know what's in that green stuff. It could be slime or puke!"

Unexpectedly, Dad's stomach began to suddenly cramp. He's been stuffing his face all day but nothing was coming out the exit.

"*Uggghhh* . . . my stomach," Dad moaned, clutching his over-sized midsection. "I really need to *poooo* . . ."

"Oh, dear," Mom muttered.

*   *   *

The drive to the supermarket was uneventful except Mom was the slowest poke on the poky road.

"Mom, you're going too slow. Go faster. Everyone is passing us!" I whined like a nine-year-old.

"Now, now . . . you make me nervous when you shout," Mom said timidly, clutching the steering wheel. "Passengers are not supposed to disturb the driver. It's against the criminal law of this country."

Mom was not confident behind the wheel but she was never involved in an accident or ever got a ticket in her thirty years of driving. Dad, on the other hand, was the most confident driver in the galaxy but his collection of moving vehicle citations could fill up moon craters.

I continued to whine and complain as car after car zipped past us. For a second I even thought I saw a classmate and tried to hide. The supermarket was probably no more than six miles away but it might take half an hour to get there. *Do the math!*

* * *

I had never spent much time in the grocery section of the supermarket. Our family was primarily an aisle and back shopper—boxed goods, canned goods, cereals, and meats.

The variety of natural colors from all kinds of fruits and vegetables was a novel experience. And for Mom too. But she poked and pinched like she was some kind of picky pro with exacting standards when actually she hadn't a clue. Potatoes she knew, but kale was a different kind of animal. No mass and body to it. Leaves? What do you do with that? Nibble?

She recalled the old days when her family used to chow down on pretty much everything, including green, red, yellow, orange, and purple vegetables, roots, and fruits. Cruciferous vegetables. Spinach. Swiss chard. Savoy cabbage. Celery. Basil leaves. But that was a long time ago when she was a little piglet in Cornwall.

I wanted to try them all. The funny looking things called artichokes. The red, squishy things called tomatoes. The pungent, white bulbs called garlic. Mom recoiled with confusion. She knew garlic bread. But just plain bulbs of garlic were something new.

Mom and I together carried a basket of all kinds of leafy greens and fruits to the checkout counter.

"My, my . . . are we having a big family get together?" the clerk asked. She was plump with a maternal silhouette.

"Ummmm, no. Just food . . . for dinner," Mom said haltingly.

"You guys eat really healthy! Good for you!"

"Oh, yes. We always try to eat the best," Mom said, lying shamelessly through her snout. She was at least seventy pounds overweight, even for a pig. She says she can't help it she has thick ankles.

"Mom, what do you mean?!" I asked, very confused.

"Hush!" she interrupted.

"But this is our first—" I was whisked away before I could finish elaborating.

"I have a school project! We normally never eat like this! —" I shouted outside the entrance like a boy being taken hostage.

* * *

About thirty minutes later, Mom and I arrived back home.

"What took you so long?!" Dad shouted between belches. He hadn't pooped yet and his body felt like an overfilled septic tank.

"Mom drives slow!" I said, stating the obvious. Redolence from Dad's internal plumbing was starting to overtake the room.

"Oh, we were shopping. It takes time when you're shopping for more than boneless rib-eye," Mom explained. She tried opening some windows to break up the strong incense. No use.

Anxious about the project, I wondered how the other kids were getting along. Did they have a big veggie meal planned like me? I wanted to go upstairs for fresh oxygen and get in touch with my classmates.

"I'll clean the veggies and cook up something tomorrow!" Mom shouted as she spotted me running up to my room.

"Thanks Mom!" I yelled.

Minutes later, the responses I got from my classmates were a little puzzling. It seemed no one was doing anything special at all.

"Having roast with cesar salid. Soft karots potatose. Mum also got bock choy," posted Mason on Snapshaft.

"Were going to soup nation and have all you can eat buffet. Will try some veggies for the report. They have delish ice cream!" wrote Asha on her Facebark page.

"Nothing special. Spageti. Tomatoes. Spinich. brocolini. Same junk!" tweezed Tim on Twizzer.

Aside from a few marginal additions to the menu, it was just the same old for most children. No one seemed to be unfamiliar with plant foods except me. *That stinks!* I thought. It didn't seem fair.

* * *

The next morning I found a kitchen full of greens, reds, oranges, and yellows.

"AAAhhhhhhhhhhhhhhhh!" Dad roared randomly.

My eyes feasted on the colors while my brain tried to interpret its meaning.

"What is all this in the kitchen? Are we turning into a giant stinkin' forest? It's smelling up the house!" he belched.

"I can't wait to eat!" I exulted.

Genetics is weird. Sometimes I wonder how I could be related. My science teacher, Mrs. Porter, says chromosomal recombination can have unexpected results. For instance, Dad has tusks. I have pink, rosy cheeks. He's rough and shaggy. I'm soft and hairless. He's all boar. The school nurse says I'm perfectly boy—and cute. He hates veggies. I can't wait to try them. Maybe Mom . . . ? Perish the thought!

"Calm down! It's just for a day or two," Mom said.

Mom used some of the recipes from my teacher but looked up a few more from the internet as well. She started to remember some of the dishes she had as an infant. She prepared tomato sauce. Salad with Italian dressing. Spinach pot pie. Steamed carrots and broccoli. Fried rice with pineapples.

Mom was a relatively bad cook but somehow she managed to whip up all kinds of dishes. But its authenticity was a different matter. None of us knew what it was supposed to taste like because recipe books don't come with flavor and smell. No one could tell whether she did a poor job or the dish was just bad from the start, confirming Dad's suspicions that "*if it ain't meat, it ain't fit to eat!*"

* * *

At dinner Dad was still in his usual foul, truculent mood.

"Gang dangit . . . *Gggggooooooooooddd!*" he yelled.

His personal septic tank was becoming more and more uncomfortable.

"Achoooo! Achooooo! *ACHHOOOOOOOOOO!*" His allergies were starting up again too.

A dinner of mostly vegetables was served for the first time in the Swine household and Dad was not very happy. There was some meats on the table, but it was paltry compared to what he was used to. Certainly, not enough to satisfy a full grown, four hundred pound warthog.

"It's just this one time, honey. Try some pumpkin and spinach. And sautéed cauliflower in sweet and sour sauce," Mom implored.

"Ahhh . . . alright. But you're to blame if I get sick!"

"You're not going to get sick, dear."

"I told you about my friend. He almost died from a bucket of coleslop."

I came down from my room and was amazed by the cornucopia of colors and vegetables of all kinds. While I didn't have the stomach size to eat it all, I wanted to have a taste of everything.

The broccoli was ticklish against the roof of my mouth.

The zucchini was soft and mushy. Pumpkin was sweet, almost like candy. And the carrots were soft and squishy. But sometimes hard. Mom was inconsistent. She also baked up some kale and they were crispy like potato chip treats. *MMmmmm . . .*

"Yummmyyy!" I exclaimed.

"Thanks, sweetie. I don't think I've ever gotten a compliment on my cooking."

"Ain't it good, Dad?" I asked. He was all frowns.

"*Arrgghhhhhhhhh!*" he shouted. "I'll manage. But I'd love a barrel of fried chicken right now."

Slowly but surely, the Swine family scarfed down the tableful of vegetables from arugula to zucchini. I flitted from plate to plate, biting a little bit here, a taste there, and a portion of something new and delicious in another part of the table.

"You're running around like a fox!" Mom said to me. "Foxes make me nervous."

"I'm trying to taste everything, Mom. I have to do a report."

Soon, the table was almost bare. And Dad, despite all his protestations, had finished almost the entire meal on his own.

"*BUUUURRRRPPPPP. BEEEEELCHHHHHHHH!*" Dad excreted. It sounded like he was finished. "I think I'm done. I can't have another bite. I probably weigh a ton."

"Did you have a favorite, dear?" Mom asked.

"Hard to say. It all tasted grassy! Mushrooms bring back memories of the time I was lost in the Piney Woods of East Texas when I was a baby. I had to scavenge for food. The tofu with black sauce was alright. I can almost taste protein. Sort of has a meaty flavor. Lentils with cumin and refried beans were okay, too."

Dad was obviously keen on protein and essential amino acids. "Maybe we'll make lentils and refried beans a regular thing," Mom said.

"But nothing compares to *STTTTEEEEAAAAAKKKK!* I want steak TOMORROWWWWW," Dad roared. "None of this SALAD CRAPALALALALALALALALALALA! *Burrrrpppp!*"

But unexpectedly, in the middle of his outburst and earsplitting screamologue, something began to transpire . . . Like a volcanic eruption, from a dormant septic tank long assumed dead.

"*Grrrrrrrrrr!*"

"What's that terrible sound?" Mom wondered aloud.

"*Booooong. Biiiing. Bbbrrrruuuuuuuuuuhiiii!*"

"What the heck?! That's more disgusting than usual! Mom, are you sure I'm not adopted?" I asked. I had to know.

"Of course, dear. Don't be silly. You're all pig, just like your dad and me," she replied. That wasn't the answer I was hoping for.

"*Guugugugugu! Guguguguguggu! Gaaagaaagaaagaa!*"

"Yuck," I yelped, with a scowl I couldn't help evince, utterly disgusted with whatever it was, whoever it was, obviously Dad. Vainly, I tried to pinch my olfactory glands, but the miasma was like tear gas. My eyes were forming pools of sad water.

Abruptly, Dad jumped from his chair and began to run. He ran like the warthog of old. Almost as if an African lion was chasing him. He ran. And ran. On all fours. Straight to the bathroom on the other side of the living room.

Mom and I looked at each other with amazement, amusement, and aversion. What had just happened? Is it possible? After nineteen days, could this be the breakthrough Dad was waiting for?

And from the most unlikely—actually likely—source. VEGETABLES! Full of fiber and other good stuff.

"Waaaahhhhhh!"

Flush!

"AAGGGGGHHHHHHHH!"

Flush!

"EEEEGGGGGGHHHHHHHHH!"

Flush!

"RELIEEEEEEEEEEFFF!"

Flush!

"HOOOOORAYYYYYYYYY!"

Flush!

Fifteen flushes in total but it felt like infinity and forever. Dad was making poo mountains in the toilet and pushing the outer limits of modern plumbing. I was afraid the sudden rearrangement of mass could put the earth's natural rotation at risk.

Almost twenty minutes later, Dad emerged from the bathroom with a big smile of relief on his face from tusk to tusk.

"Yaahhhoooooooooooooooooooooooo!"

"Feeling better, dear?" Mom asked rhetorically. Of course he was feeling better.

"Sure am . . . finally got it done," Dad announced proudly.

"It was probably those vegetables," I remarked.

"No, I did it!" Dad refuted strongly. "I pushed it down! My body had enough of the *krayola* and pushed it all out!"

Privately, however, Dad knew the vegetables had worked its magic, as they usually do. The fiber in the carrots, kale, spinach, broccoli, asparagus, and a myriad of other greens, yellows, and reds acted like a sewer snake in Dad's very bloated, distended, and jammed intestinal plumbing system.

He was pleased as well even if he wouldn't admit it openly. His septic tank was cleaned out. And that should mean fewer unwelcome eruptions throughout the house.

"You want me to make more vegetables for dinner?" Mom asked.

"Let's not get carried away, but I'm okay . . . with an occasional lettuce leaf," Dad answered reticently.

In coming days Dad adopted changes, albeit small, on the heels of the gastronomic miracle that will probably go down in Swine family lore.

A bit of veggies were added in between mammoth slabs of steak. He wasn't going to cut back on meat—no chance of that—but he was willing to help wash it down with some kale and asparagus from time to time. Just to clean out the plumbing, he said. A precautionary, safety measure. Plumbers do it all the time, he explained.

* * *

I presented my school report and it was one of the best in class. I was rewarded with applauds and ovations from the other kids punctuated by burps from a couple smart alecks, which I didn't appreciate. More importantly, I earned an A+ for content, creativity, and effort. Ms. Jones was impressed with my exuberance for something as mundane as plain squash.

She said I helped the class see vegetables like it was for the very first time. For me, it really was. "Plant shapes and colors erupted from Sam's presentation, reminding us of exotic candies, distant stars and crazy monsters," praised Ms. Jones. Her lofty encomium almost made me turn radish red.

Speaking before the class was a little nerve-wracking but I ate my greens and got through it. It didn't give me superhuman strength but downing a can of spinach in one gulp like Popeye was a funny ice breaker.

"Cherry tomatoes exploded in my mouth like warm grenades," I told the class in my oral presentation. And "asparagus resemble spears that could lance aliens from cauliflower planets." I probably went a little over the top. My imagination can be bananas.

My classmates also learned valuable lessons from Dad's experience as well. Vegetables are not just tasty, but important for overall good health and feelings of wellness

As the ancient Greek doctor Hippocrates once said, "All disease begins in the gut." What goes into your stomach inevitably redounds back to you. That might be in the form of a healthy, sound physical body. Or like my dad, clogged plumbing that leaves you stuffed and feeling irritated.

3

OPENERS & CLOSERS

*"Idiosyncrasies can seem charming in the beginning.
Eventually, it's just annoying."*

Mom is what you might call an *opener*. She likes to leave everything open—lids, boxes, doors, windows, cabinets, bags . . . Everything must be in the ajar and unclosed position.

Our kitchen, for instance, swings with open cabinet doors and pulled out drawers. Plastic lids are never quite locked in tight. Bags of chips are unsealed. Our refrigerator is full of open cartons and half closed containers. The result is stale chips and a very stinky frig. *Yuck!*

When it's warm, she doesn't just open a few windows. She opens every window in the house. Even her private moments are shared publicly. When she goes to the bathroom, the door is unclosed. Agape. Oftentimes open all the way. She doesn't seem to mind that she's sitting on the toilet in full view. Maybe it's claustrophobia. Or it helps her to feel connected to the entire world. I'm just a kid. It's hard to figure out these things. But Dad says he doesn't have the answers, either. I imagine that when she was younger she was more modest. I can't be sure.

Curiously, Dad is the exact opposite. He's what you might call a *closer*. Everything must be tightly shut—windows, doors, lids, cabinets, and boxes. When he enters a room, he shuts the door behind him. When he leaves a room, he locks the door after him. Not shut? Half closed? It's one of the worst things you could possibly do. It drives him crazy. Because of Mom, he's always running through the kitchen shutting drawers and cabinet doors. He wants them "closed!" he squawks. "*Bbbuuuuurrppp!*"

As for me, I seem to have gotten a little of both from Mom and Dad. Sometimes I leave things open. Sometimes I close them. And many times that gets me into trouble depending on who's hovering over me.

"You left the cabinet door open!" Dad once reprimanded. "Close it! Pronto, buster!"

"But I'm still using it, Dad!" I demurred.

"No! Close it NOW!" he ordered.

In the winter, the windows had to be completely shut. That's good when it's chilly outside, but that habit also carries over into the warm summers as well which drives Mom insane. She wants to feel the breeze traveling through the living room. It reminds her of open prairies and bucolic hills, she says. For Dad, the only breeze he wants to feel seems to be the warm gale of his belches and booms rushing through the halls.

* * *

The weather has been very strange lately. In the day, it feels like the Mojave Desert. By evening, it's Siberian winter. Dad said the thermostat varied as much as forty degrees. Intemperate, barbarian weather was laying siege to the house. Fluctuations from day to night had become so drastic we were facing a domestic crisis. Mom and Dad are bickering like two enemy piglets because someone left the windows open or shut. It makes you wonder how the two ever got married. Do opposites really attract? Or just get into endless arguments?

While the feud, on the surface, might seem like a simple difference of opinion, in reality, it was the age old clash of the *openers* and *closers*. Like sectarian rivals, Mom and Dad were each convinced that their way was the orthodox truth and the other side was heresy.

"Achooo!" I think I might be catching a cold. Children aren't meant for extreme weather. I'm not a feral animal, after all. I'm as domesticated as little kids come.

"Honey, I'm freezing! You left all the windows open. Again!" Dad yelled. *"Arrggghhhhhh!"*

Idiosyncrasies can seem charming in the beginning. I imagine that's the way it was with Mom and Dad when they first met. One said *tomāto*. The other said *tomäto*. Eventually, it's just annoying.

"Then close them, dear" Mom quipped. Of course, she'd open it as soon as he closed it.

It was 8 p.m. and the house felt like the outside of an igloo. I was freezing, too, but I saw the cold as a savage force of nature, not the consequence of an eccentric mother that had all the windows open in the house. I did my best to manage with extra socks, sweats, and shirts. But by now, my nose was beginning to run like the Mississippi in summer and mosquitoes were buzzing in my head.

"*Yaaaaaaaaggghhhh!*" arose a frustrated scream.

The new Swine ritual seemed to be that Dad shut the windows at night, which meant every window in the house. And by 7 a.m. following morning, every window was opened again. Dad was freezing. Mom was hot. I was both and stuck in between. It's not easy being in a mixed family.

"Mom, can't you and Dad be reasonable about this? Do you have to open and close every window?" I asked.

"I like the cool breeze," she replied. "I like the windows open. I'm a pig. We're pigs. We have extra fat around the bones. We need natural cooling."

But I was a skinny kid. I didn't inherit mom's corpulent genes. I had no extra protection. My bones were exposed.

"Your dad is crazy!" she complained. "He wants everything closed even when it's hot. Maybe savanna warthogs are built a little differently from the English. I don't know. But I don't like my neck all hot and sweaty."

"Mom, I think I might be catching a cold. I'm not used to extreme weather. It's so hot during the day. And so cold at night. I'm not a wild animal."

"Blame your father, dear. Fresh air is good for you. Warm, stuffy air will make anyone sick."

"*Achooo!*" I think I was getting really sick. "*Achooo! Achooo!*"

"Geez, Sam. You're almost as loud as your father," Mom groused.

"*YAAAHHHH!*" Dad yelled from the safety of his hermetically sealed room. "Did someone say something?!" Dad was in retreat, immured in his chamber. He could make sure the windows in his room were closed, but not the windows throughout the house. That was a question of perseverance. And Mom was more determined.

"No, dear!" Mom shouted. "Now, sit next to the window, honey, and get some fresh air," she exhorted. "That should clear up your stuffiness. Always works for me!"

*   *   *

By the following day, I had a full blown cold. The temperature in my ear was 105 degrees. The doctor said I had a high-grade fever.

"Is that really bad?" I squeaked.

"Well, son. Not so good. But you'll get better with lots of soup and rest."

Privately, the good doctor told my mom and dad that the temperature in the house was too erratic. It should be around seventy-eight degrees, he recommended. No extreme temperatures. No radical changes. It's not good for a child, he said. It shouldn't be too cold. Nor too hot. Moderation was important.

"My wife, she's the darnedest woman, Doc!" Dad moaned. "She opens all the windows. And you know how cold it gets in the evenings these days. It's freezing!"

"No, that's not true, Doctor!" Mom countered. "He closes all the windows. And you know how hot it gets during the day. It's no wonder Sam is sick. A boy needs fresh air."

"You can't open all the windows!"

"You can't close all the windows!"

"It's cold! The windows have to be closed!"

"Too cold for you is anything below eighty degrees. You should try wearing a sweater!"

"Now, here, here!" the doctor interrupted, struggling to calm the situation. "Let's try to be reasonable. We're talking about your child's well-being. He's not a farm animal, you know."

Mom and Dad stared at each other and exchanged quizzical looks. They weren't sure what to make of that.

"I mean, he's not a lion or bear," the doc restated.

"No, he sure ain't!" they blurted out.

"He's a little boy. He's domesticated," continued the doctor. "He could never survive in the wild. The ambient temperature indoor should be moderate and comfortable. Please . . . If you two don't settle this, he'll only get more sick."

"Okay. Sorry, Doctor," Dad said. "I'll make sure *Mrs. Swine* doesn't open all the windows."

"Yes, Doctor. And I'll make sure *Mr. Swine* doesn't close all the windows!"

"Very good. Now, I'll be back in a few days to check up on Sam. I hope you two keep to your promises. Or else Sam will really get sick," the doctor warned. "And you know what happens to sick children . . ."

What?

*   *   *

Promises were easier made than kept. Partisan squabbling continued over the next couple days. Each side accused the other of apostasy and heterodoxy. They were like religious zealots firmly holding to canon. Maybe I was being punished for their sins?

"The doctor said we have to be reasonable. I left a handful of windows open!" Dad snorted.

"Just a handful? We need at least a baker's dozen!" Mom sneered.

"It's too cold for Sam!"

"No, it wasn't too cold. The thermostat was seventy-eight on the dot!"

"Yes, after I closed the windows you had opened!"

"That's the most ridiculous thing I ever heard!"

"You're the most ridiculous woman!"

"That's so rude! And you think you're a gentleman? You lout!"

The arguing continued to spiral down. Ecumenical understanding seemed impossible. Eventually they huffed and puffed and withdrew to their private quarters. If they could, they would have built separation barriers between them.

BANG! Dad shut the door behind him. "*Meshugana!*" he roared.

Mom went into her room and left her door wide open. Her windows, too, because she needed the fresh air. "*Majnoon!*" she yelled.

*   *   *

A few neighbors came to visit. Ms. Murphy from across the street brought cookies and chicken soup. She visited with her six-year-old daughter named Molly. Her face was dotted with brown freckles and her red hair was braided on either side of her head. She looked like Pippi Longstocking. We played retro games like Chutes N' Ladders and Connect Four. I let her win sometimes and she was very happy.

"Yay! I won!" she shouted, jumping around the room.

"Yes, you did, Molly. You're so smart!" I said.

"What kind of game is this?" she asked. Physical board games and tactile objects were foreign to her. She only knew *apps.*

"Old games our parents used to play in the Paleolithic." Artifacts of an ancient past.

"Paleo—*what?*"

We also watched some videos of cats and puppies on WeTube. It's amazing how many videos there are of cats and puppies. Pets peddle in cute like stores offloading shoes at ninety percent off. There's no way kids can compete. If animals could talk, parents wouldn't have children.

Mrs. Chao from the PTA dropped by as well to see if I was strong enough to do some homework in bed. She thought I was a good student and didn't want to see me falling behind. "University is just around the corner," she would say.

She has a son named Billy in the eighth grade who already takes college level math. He passed two high school AP exams and scored perfectly on the PSAT. Still, she's afraid Harbard won't accept him because of his background notwithstanding the stellar record and extracurriculars up the wazoo.

"No, no . . . I'm too sick . . . I can't do any homework," I weakly murmured, pretending to be super uber ill.

Last summer Billy helped Burmese farmers turn salt water into fresh. The summer before that, he helped Peruvian peasants in the Andes capture sunlight for electricity. This year, the plan is to help refugees in Yemen, Syria or Libya. There's no guarantee he'll come back.

"My, my . . . you are a sick little boy. I hope there will be a renascent interest in your studies soon. I can't believe your parents can be so pococurante," she said, peppering her sentences intentionally with words no one understood.

The vocabulary was above my grade, but I think I got the gist of it through tone and context. My parents were still fighting tooth and hoof and couldn't figure out how to compromise. Interfaith dialog isn't easy. We could hear them shouting down the hall.

"No, it's your fault! You're the bad one!" Mom squealed.

"No, it's not my fault. It's your fault! You're bad!" Dad hollered back.

"You think more about yourself than your own child!"

"You care more about your flowers than your husband!"

"Your yelling drives people crazy!"

"Your mud baths stink up the house!"

"I'm British! What are you?"

"I'm warthog! My family fought in the civil war!"

"Americans are uncouth and pushy!"

I wasn't just sick anymore. By now, buzzing mosquitoes had moved to my ear and were giving me an ear ache.

"Compromise is important if we want to get along," Mrs. Chao quietly shared. "Fanaticism leads to acrimony. There's a place for dogmatism—doing well in school—but in most cases, we should be flexible. Forbearance is a virtue. We ought to pursue a broadminded *Weltanschauung*."

"Aren't you afraid Billy could be captured?" I asked.

"There's a one in 221,839 chance."

My chums, Danny and Scott, also came by to tell me what was going on at school. Danny said the algebra test was hard but he'd clue me in on the questions. Scott said the kids were getting together to form a basketball team. When I get better, I could join in.

The guys and I talked a while, threw some football in the room and played with darts and other kinds of throwing weapons. I had toy shurikens, knives, and miniature spears. However, Danny missed the board a couple times and darts flew out the open window. They almost hit Mrs. Chao and Ms. Murphy on the head who were chatting outside.

"*Agggghhhhhhhhhh!*" they screamed.

"You kids almost impaled us with spears!" scolded Mrs. Chao.

Wow! That should be illegal, I thought to myself.

"Close that window! And you shouldn't play with knives!" Ms. Murphy yelled.

"Sorry!" Danny shouted. "We didn't mean to skewer you!"

Almost killing someone was frightening but sort of funny too. It's a strange paradox. Are humor and horror the inverse of each other like reflections in a distorted mirror? The terrifying and humorous often feel equally unreal but for opposite reasons.

"In a different dimension of the multiverse, we're being hauled off in handcuffs," Scott hypothesized.

"Ms. Murphy would have a dart in her ear," said Danny.

"How come all the interesting stuff only happens in other dimensions?" I asked.

They shrugged their shoulders. It was one of those universal mysteries. Other worlds always seemed more interesting than this one.

* * *

Missing school has its benefits but lying in bed alone wasn't that much fun. But with everything at your fingertips, I wasn't missing too much. Internet in Suidae Valley was still on the slower side, but it was faster than old fashioned dial up.

Scott sent videos of well-wishers from school. They goofed and asked if I had the Bubonic plague. Danny told them that we impaled Mrs. Chao with darts and she had to go to the hospital. Scott said we were almost hauled off to prison but he talked the police out of it. The past was the multiverse.

Teachers messaged me as well. Ms. Jones, my health class teacher, reminded me to get plenty of lemon juice and water. She said electrolytes are important for a sickly child. I asked if I could substitute lemon juice with soda. Sodas have a lot of fizz that appear charged with electricity. She said sodas are charged with sugars and acids like phosphate that will rot my mouth. I should stay away if I still want teeth at sixty. But sixty seemed like a long time away. I wanted to enjoy my cold glass of soda *now!*

My history teacher, Mr. Johnson, said I was missing his best lectures yet—the great Julius Caesar. He said Caesar conquered the world before the age of thirty. I told him I still had lots of time left. But time flies, he warned. His childhood feels like yesterday. Where had it all gone? Life is fugacious. Maybe time is just an illusion of the mind, I offered. Perhaps there's no time at all? We invented time to explain *change*. He said I might be on to something. I wasn't sure what I was on to, but I tried holding my breath and walking backwards, but no luck turning back the clock.

Ms. Fearstein said I was failing English. She said that if I wanted academic reprieve, I'd have to bring a notarized medical note from my doctor. She said she didn't believe I was really sick. She wasn't sure if I was even human. I sent her pictures of me lying in bed and video clips of the doctor examining me. But she can't be fooled, she jeered. She's familiar with every trick in the book. It's a dusty old book.

Mr. McCoy, my math teacher, congratulated me on my

successful abstention. He said that in the real world more of something is not always additive. More could actually be deductive. That's why people take vacations. He asked if I was enjoying my vacation. I told him being forced to lie in the supine position with a 105 degree temperature was ruining my holiday. He messaged me back and said people sometimes die on vacations.

*   *   *

Over the next several days, my cold gradually improved, thankfully, though the theological discord between my parents continued to simmer. They learned to compromise a little, but they often tried to cheat when they thought the *other* wasn't looking. Trickery, artifice, and ruse abounded, both sides apparently cohering to the credo, *"By way of deception."* They didn't seem to think integrity was important when the other side was unequivocally wrong.

"Honey, I see you trying to open that window," Dad said. "You can't fool me!"

"No . . . I was just checking to see if it was stuck. Besides, I saw you try to close the window in Sam's room and it was over eighty-two degrees in there!"

"The weather was turning cold. I was just being cautious."

"You're trying to cheat! Hoodwinker!"

"Don't call me a cheat. You dubious trickster!"

The weather also improved unexpectedly, which probably deserves the most credit. Sometimes, when headstrong parents can't agree, Mother Nature intervenes. The temperature turned salutary and with it my fever as well. After a week, I was back to my salubrious self again and the doctor gave me a clean bill of health. All was forgiven.

"You're as fit as a guitar," the doctor said.

"Is that anything like a fiddle?" I asked.

"Oh yes, even better. Guitars are more versatile."

"Thanks, Doc!" Dad interjected. "You're even better than the family vet we used to have when I was a kid."

"I do try my best to take care of everyone," the doctor said.

"I know it's all our fault," Mom declared. "Sometimes I wonder how Sam survives in this house. It can feel like a barn."

"You have—ahem—a *lovely* home, Mrs. Swine"

"Can I get a notarized medical note?" I begged, remembering that I needed to get an excuse for school.

"Why in the world for?" the doctor asked.

"My teacher, Ms. Fearstein, thinks I'm not sick. She's not even sure I'm human. She says she's going to fail me!"

"Don't worry, Sam. I'll take care of her."

Things in the Swine household soon returned to normal. Windows in the house were inappropriately open or closed. The refrigerator reeked of yesterday's dinner, lunch, and breakfast, and a sundry other left-overs. Random bags of cookies and chips were torn open or sealed tightly shut. The windows in my room mysteriously opened and closed on their own depending on which parent came in to check.

And despite the temporary truce between the *openers* and *closers*, I saw no lasting detente between opposing sides.

Perhaps these differences are irreconcilable? Manichean worldviews can be hard to resolve. Creeds weren't meant to be negotiable. Or maybe they get along better in other dimensions of the multiverse where Mrs. Chao and Ms. Murphy are impaled and recovering in hospital beds. I hope they get better soon.

4

SPIDERBOY

*"The liquor is sweet like fermented
nectar. Wine of the gods."*

There was nothing but vast, pale landscape. In the corner emanated light. I scrambled forward. To the left. Back. To the right. Diagonally. I paused to rest. *Where am I?* I scrambled back. To the left. Forward. To the right. I was frantic. *Where to go?* Everything was upside down. More than half a dozen spindly legs extended out from underneath me.

I was dreaming I was a spider.

Instinctively, I ejected a silk-like rope from behind and plunged downward. The world was right-side up again.

A gentle breeze rocked me to and fro, and the world seemed to move. I hung from my line like an expert trapeze artist. Over to the side was a dark figure near the glowing light. It was a large, hairy creature. I wasn't sure what it was, but it frightened me.

Suddenly it moved and two bulging eyes seemed to look straight at me. Uh oh! I've been found out! Somehow I knew.

Quickly I tried to scramble up my line but a horrible boom from the beast shook the earth and me with it.

I swung like a space monkey in the air and then my line unexpectedly snapped! Down . . . down . . . down I went . . . *CRASH!* I hit the floor with a thump. Strange. It didn't hurt.

I scrambled. Run! Run! Run! The ground quaked as the beast jumped about in search of its prey. I presume, little ol' me!

I found a black crevice underneath an obstruction and squeezed myself in. Safety. For now. The beast bellowed! *"Arrggghhh!"* The sound was horrible. It picked up an ominous red canister and began to spray everywhere. The air became toxic. I couldn't breathe. It was a chemical attack. Gas. Sarin. Weapons of mass destruction. Why isn't this illegal? I was on the verge of dying. Vertigo. Consciousness *fading . . .*

* * *

Luckily, the nerve gas didn't kill me. I recovered. My lungs were powerful. I was safe for now. The beast had retreated. Illumination filled the room. I couldn't see exactly what was around me, but there seemed to be an instinctive sense for my surroundings. The enclosure was ginormous. I wasn't alone. It belonged to someone. It did not welcome my presence.

Hungry. I felt so hungry. But what do I eat? I wanted to eat anything. Alive. Juicy. Moths. Flies. Ants. Mosquitoes. Worms. *Gross!* But there was a craving that was undeniable. Inevitable. I was famished. Irresistible.

I began to climb. Higher ground. Had to get to higher ground. And a corner. Need some kind of nook. An angle. Need to make a web. A snare. And my home. Need to build. Weave a web.

I worked hard and tirelessly. Assiduously. Round and round I went. I jumped and climbed. I crawled and ran. My eight spindly legs worked in perfect unison. From behind, I released a viscid line that was the raw material for my trap and my new home. Around and around I continued to go. I was exhausted. It felt like hours. But eventually, I was finished. My masterpiece. My beautiful web. My creation. Poetry. Heaven. Marvelous.

I inspected every millimeter. And from my new outpost, I gazed out into the world. I sensed the breeze. Odd smells. Vibrations. Indistinct. Sounds. Noises. Insects buzzing from afar. Exotic creatures moving about. Space teeming with life. And I waited. I had time. I wanted to rest. I was so tired.

* * *

Suddenly, the lines shook. Intruder! It was a fly! I think. It buzzed like a desperate lunatic. It was stuck. My meal. Food! Grub! Finally. So hungry. Starved. I quickly attacked and spun my web around and around my victim. It struggled maniacally. It looked at me with its thousand eyes. Forlorn. What a strange creature. Bizarre. Freakish. It wanted to live. I wanted it *dead!* Still. Lifeless. Soon, it became nearly quiet. It was rolled in a cocoon of web. I inserted my teeth into its leathery skin, puncturing it. *Yum* . . . I drank. Drank. Drank. *Mmmmmm* . . . The fountain of life. Elixir. I was gorged. Satiated. I felt myself growing stronger.

Now it was time to rest. My abdomen was full. Life was good. It was perfect. Everything was *just as it should be.* Wonderful!

Then the lights came on. The beast had returned!

"Buuuurrrp!" it announced shamelessly. Effulgent light invaded the room. Everything radiated like the moon and sun. Brilliant. Resplendent. The sound of fizz. Soda. Beer. Then the television. Men swinging sticks. Balls flying. Cheers. *"RRRAAAHHHHHWWW!"* A riot of sounds.

The tumult was terrifying. Petrifying. What is it? Where did it come from? The noise? They seemed both familiar and unfamiliar. But I think I'm safe here. I hope I'm safe here. This is my domain. My sphere. My world. My territory. If the beast comes for me again, he'll be entrapped in my web! I hope. No, it's too big. I need a bigger web. I need a matrix of hemp and steel.

I dozed off.

* * *

In the background, there was chatter between the beast and a pig. Arguments. Oinks. Squeals. Grunts. Foul odor. Effluvium. Eccentric smells. Stench. Oh no! Where was I? What sort of hell is this? Why was I reborn here? The gods are cruel!

Ahaahh! Another victim! This time an ant. This critter thought he could trespass through my territory. But now it was trapped. I swiftly ran towards it. It was a worker ant. Maybe a scout. Sad little thing. Morose. It looked exhausted. Maybe it had been in search of food for hours? Now it was food. It seemed to beg for mercy. But no mercy for thee! It shook its mandibles in mock attack. I put it in chains. It was secure. But I was still full from my last meal. I would save this one for later. The ant was still alive. Fresh meat. Kosher. Halaal.

Now back to sleep. Why was I so sleepy? Spiders sleep a lot. Or maybe it remains in an unconscious state to conserve energy. I don't know. It's just a dream. I'm imagining all of this. It's not real. I think it's a dream, right? *Who am I? Where did I come from?* Why am I putting insects in bondage and liking it? Why am I eating bugs? Why am I so hungry? Was I born this way?

* * *

Most times are uneventful. I sit for hours in *pseudo* meditation. If I were human I would be *ersatz* bodhisattva, except I don't want to save all beings. I want to eat them. I'm nearly comatose but fully awake. Just waiting. Biding my time. Perfectly happy to be still. No thinking. No wanting. No craving. Sometimes I go out to inspect my terrain. I clean up debris and push aside dried discard. Old cargo must go. There's no room for dated meat.

I travel far beyond my domain. I explore the vast frontier. I've been to the kitchen. I've traveled into the darkness. The damp basement underneath. The dusty garage on the other side of the world. It's fecund with activity. The remains of the dead are everywhere. Fossils. Skeletons. Mass graves. Danger lurks all around.

My honeycomb of silk and rope resonate with the motion of the room. I read it like a telegraph. I collect information like a news reporter. It's a radar. A stethoscope. My palace of web is an extension of my body. A byzantine bridge between the world and my self.

At sunrise when the light shines softly on the delicate silky lattice still moist from the morning dew, the view on the horizon is a thing of sublime beauty. At that moment there is a still, quiet peace that descends on everything in the universe. In the distant corner is the silhouette of an animal, the head of a desiccated ant. It's my Mona Lisa.

* * *

There was a flurry of activity in the kitchen. It's the pig. Raw bovine carcass burned on the grill. A jumbo roast. She lumbered hither and thither leaving muddy tracks on the ground. She gave out a snort. It was a call to the beast. It barreled into the room. It demanded meat. Steak. Food. It's gruff. Gauche. Crude. Truculent. *"Noowwww!"* it roared. A fusillade of mad oinks and grunts followed. Barrage of noisy exchanges. And then it took a seat at the table. It's heaving. Agitated. Restless.

The pig has forgotten something. In search, she plods in my direction. Uh oh! I retreat into my barrack. My organic cockpit. My latticework of web shook violently as she passed. Seismic activity. She leaves behind a bouquet of stink that hangs in the air. She finds plates buried under laundry and turns back for the kitchen. But she spots me. She knows I'm here. Discovered. She shakes her head. Oinks. Curious for a moment. But then disinterested. Forgotten. She has bigger meat to spear.

The roast is ready and grilled bovine carcass is served on over-sized plates. The air is redolent with the aroma of charcoal and burned flesh. The beast assaults the dead animal. He tears it into pieces. Poor cow. It's a hyenic feeding frenzy. It seems to go on for hours.

Many minutes pass. Quiet settled the room. Repose. Calm. It's dark outside. Night penetrated the interior. Occupants have retreated to their separate chambers. Peace. Stillness. I'm safe. I return to my leftover kill. The liquor is sweet like fermented nectar. Wine of the gods. I offer a swig to Bacchus.

* * *

Oh no! The beast is on the move again. Why can't it stay still? Or go away?! His two bulging eyes have spotted me. I'm found again. It appears upset. Very upset. It's angry! Enraged!

It's looking for something. Chemical weapons? Nerve gas? A big stick? It's frantic.

It lifted a newspaper from the table and rolls it into a cudgel. No! Have mercy, ugly beast! I'm just a tiny spider. I don't take up much space!

Run! Run! I must run! I ran across the vast, great, white plain as fast as I can. My legs carry me furiously like limbs allegro concerto.

The beast swings . . .

Thump! It missed me.

Thump! It missed me, again.

Then, *thump!* It got me!

I fall. Fall. Fall. Fall . . .

"Oh no!"

KABOOM! I landed on the hard floor. My limbs allegro couldn't move. They're crooked. Misshapen. Octaplegic. Cruel world.

Why? Was I meant to end up like this? Was it destiny? Fate? Kismet? Or poor decision making? *Who* is dreaming this?

Then a giant, hairy hoof began to come down, down, down, down, down, down, down, down, down, down . . .

"No, Dad! . . . Don't squish me!" I cried. "Mom, help!"
Bbbbllllaaaaaaaaaaaaaaaaaaaaaaaattttt!

I was dead. Flattened like pancakes.

5

GREEN COWS & LOTTERY TICKETS

"Sometimes, you just gotta say, what the HECK!"

My dad says playing the lottery is one of those things that makes you feel stupid if you do and stupid that you didn't when you hear the news that someone won the fifty million dollar jackpot that should be yours if only you had played. The lottery is a form of legalized gambling that steals from the public. The very people the government should look out for and represent, it regressively exploits most of all. Needless to say, it's a racket.

But in exchange for a few dinars, you get the chance to win millions of dollars, except the odds are less than one in three hundred million. But who cares about statistics when you're having so much fun and regret of missing out can be avoided by taking part in the officially sanctioned robbery of the masses. Robin Hood in reverse. Or maybe there's a way to beat the political boondoggle? My dad seems to think so.

We were at the mini mart because he was feeling lucky. I reminded him how stupid it was and there was better chance of finding a hundred dollar bill on the ground than winning. He looked down—*nope!*—and then recounted his dream of green cows last night.

"Green cows are good luck," he declared. "Lotteries are dumb, but green cows are smart!" And propitiously instead of saying, *moo*, it said, *money*. All night he heard, *moo-ney. Moo-ney. Moo-ney.* It was the craziest thing. And it was a sure, auspicious sign to buy lottery tickets, he argued.

A few days ago I had a dream about being a spider. Maybe it contained a hidden message as well? "Dad, I dreamt I was a spider! Does that mean anything?" I asked.

"Yeah, it means you're gonna get squashed!" he snorted.

Not quite as benign as green cows, it seemed. "By what? A car? Falling asteroid?"

"A crazy goat! How would I know? I ain't no dream expert!"

Mom thought Dad's dream was just upset stomach from bad guacamole from the Mexican restaurant. He was moaning all night rather than the usual noisy mumblings about the guy who ripped him off and the friend who still owes him money after twenty years. Other people sleepwalk. My dad talks to himself and yells at imaginary people at 3 a.m.

The mini mart is a fun place to hang out because it's like a small grocery store, plus cheese nachos, hot dogs, and ice slurpees. They also have rubber toys at the checkout and cheap imported sunglasses for ninety-nine cents. If you wear them outside and look directly into the sun, you could burn your eyes out, my dad said. But the hot dogs are indestructible. They last forever. Mini mart snacks are perfect kids' food.

My friend, Danny, said they once found a dead rat in the hot dog machine. They're not sure if it died from the heat or hot dog. He might have a way with tall tales. Danny also claims hot dogs were once really made from dogs. Little, brown chihuahuas. And might even be still. Maybe ten percent.

When it was Dad's turn at the cashier, he threw a pair of nine-nine cent sunglasses on the counter and asked for fifty dollars in lottery tickets. They were the scratch and sniff kind. Actually, you're not supposed to sniff it but I've seen weird people do it.

"I had a dream about green cows!" he shouted at the tall, wiry cashier. "It kept saying *moo-ney!*, *moo-ney!* in my sleep."

The cashier politely nodded but didn't seem very interested. He must have heard it all. "Cool, bruh. Awesome tusks," he offered.

Dad turned to me and asked if I wanted something. A slurpee? Nachos? Hot dogs? *Chihuahua?*

I was already prepared. There was a hot dog in my left hand, nachos in my right, and a large, blue slurpee perilously perched in between.

"How about lottery tickets too?" I asked. I was feeling

lucky. It's not everyday a kid can stuff himself with mini mart junk food.

"So, you wanna play, huh? Turn your nachos into millions? Parlay your cheese? But you'll probably come up with snake eyes. I told you how stooopid gambling is."

"Yeah, I know. But I'm feeling lucky too," I said. "In my dream I ate flies and ants."

"You what?! Okay. Sure. Why not? It's not kosher, but we've never been observant. We're bacon folks through and through," he joked, turning to the cashier for a response. But nothing registered.

"Whatever you win, Sam, is all yours," he continued. "Except if it's over a thousand. Then it's half-half, partner!"

"Sure, Dad," I said, smacking my blue slurpee lips. "Steal from poor children."

He bought a few dozen lottery tickets and tossed a couple to me. We made our way to a counter at the side of the store and Dad pulled out two quarters from his pocket. He handed one to me, gesturing that we're supposed to use these to scratch the cards. Dad began to scratch and sniff furiously. I went at a more leisurely pace. No sniffing. After all, I had just two tickets. I wanted to enjoy every *umami* moment. I wanted the lottery to be as savory as the hot dog and cheese.

"Uh oh." My first ticket came up empty. *Snake eyes. Zippo. Not very fun,* I thought. I'm a sucker.

But my second ticket rewarded me a nice little prize. One hundred dollars! And I almost spilled my blue slurpee on my shirt.

"Wow! I won! I won!" I shouted. "It's my lucky day!" It felt almost like Las Vegas, except it was the mini mart. The lanky cashier gave me a thumbs up and an approving grin.

I looked over and Dad was still scratching away. All grimace. Sweat was dripping from his snout like broken nozzles. It didn't seem he was having much luck. He kept scratching and sniffing as if he was onto something. Some believe a warthog's nose is almost as sensitive as a beagle's. If only the stubborn cards would give up its secrets.

Eventually, he was down to his last two tickets and the floor was covered with the mutilated carnage of his losers. The cashier shook his head and looked at us with dismay. It seems it wasn't Dad's lucky day after all. Only mine.

"Look, I won $100!" I said.

"Good for you . . ." he mumbled. He didn't have time for Cracker Jack prizes. He was trapped in an existential calamity and he sniffed at the tickets as if there was something in the scent that held the clues to all the problems in his life. But nothing. Zippo.

His large shoulders slouched over. He felt defeated. He lost faith in the green cow and his dream. He didn't have the courage to face the last two remaining tickets and the secrets they held. He was afraid to find out. He thought he'd rather give up now than face certain disappointment.

"Here, Sam. You take 'em," he said, looking beaten. He was disconsolate. He was giving up. "You seem to be having some luck. Take a crack. I'm done."

The green cow was a false sign. No money after all.

* * *

On the drive home, Dad almost hit a family of raccoons crossing the road. Worse, he swerved and then nearly ran over an elderly woman. Luckily he stopped just inches away from her frail, bent body. Dad tried to apologize but she glared at us with very angry eyes that reminded me of Ms. Fearstein, the meanest teacher at my school. Ms. Fearstein has eyeballs that penetrate and burrow holes into your head like hot Bavarian iron. My poor head would sometimes feel like it was on fire. Her teaching license should be revoked.

When Dad tried to drive around her she shuffled over to his side and lectured him for almost five minutes about the importance of safe driving and steadfastly keeping his eyes on the road.

"Young man, this is America. You can't drive like that!" she howled.

"Sorry, mam. There were raccoons—"

"I don't know where you're from, but you can't drive the way you do over there!"

"I'm from here, mam. My ancestors fought in the Civil War. And I didn't hit you. Bye!"

Dad was so dejected and flustered he couldn't say much in his defense. What could he say anyway? He almost ran over an old lady to avoid a family of masked urban rats.

The woman also had a cane and was looking for a pretext to swing it over his head. Dad could impale her with his long tusks, but he wasn't looking for a fight. He was too glum and confused. What did the green cow mean? Why did it say, "moo-ney?" Was he just another stupid lottery sucker? He began to question his miserable life.

* * *

At the home front, Dad remained uncharacteristically quiet. No loud booms. No grunts. No random screaming. The house was eerily calm. I liked it.

Mom asked if he was hungry, but he apparently lost his appetite as well. He lied in his room staring at shadows on the wall. He moped inside the house or sniffed around the yard like an herbivore. He checked the grass. Chewed on dandelions. And mowed the lawn. He appeared to look over the horizon and contemplate, *what's it all about?*

Mom said that maybe the cows meant that he should have a steak. "This is USDA prime beef T-bone steak, honey!"

"No, I'm not hungry."

"You've gotta eat something."

"No, I don't."

"Huh? You'll starve to death!"

"Not really."

"Then have some steamed sweet potatoes."

"Not nec'ssary. We warthogs can go for days without food."

He was right, but was Dad showing signs of depression? Mom was growing concerned. Pigs usually don't get depressed. They eat. That's what keeps them happy. Mom was never depressed. She made sure of that. She always stayed fully jammed.

What could snap Dad out of his funk? Nepenthe for his

sorrows? Unfortunately, we couldn't conjure millions or win the next lottery. Even if we did, it wouldn't be his winning. Dad couldn't understand how it went wrong.

"Moo-ney," he mumbled. "Moo-ney."

Green cows and *moo-ney*.

*   *   *

I was keeping my winning ticket as a souvenir. I had a folder for these sorts of things. Report cards. Second place blue ribbon. Certificates of excellence. Old baby photos. Super hero cards. A silver buffalo coin. Honor society letters. My winning lottery ticket would serve as a nice non-academic addition. Maybe it'll mark the beginning of my future as a tycoon.

I wasn't sure what to do with my hundred dollars. I could get some new sneakers. Buy some gold and bury it in the backyard. Or maybe I should take my chances with penny stocks. Or cryptocurrencies. I'm a boy of the future. Digital money will probably become the norm by the time I grow up. Might as well get in on it when I'm young. Or I could put it in a savings account and earn .001 percent.

My history teacher said a hundred dollars is a lot of money for a kid my age. He said I made more money than most people in the world who earn less than a dollar a day. In some parts of the world, I'd be considered a rich man.

"Go abroad and retire!" Mr. Johnson joked.

"Really, I asked? Can I do that?"

"Sure, Sam. Moved to Tonga and live like a king!"

"C'mon! You're joshing. Can I really?"

"You can hire a dozen servants and go to school online. We'll save a seat right here for you. Put up a computer terminal. You can join us for class everyday."

"I have one thousand dollars in my college fund, Mr. Johnson!" a girl shouted. Her name was Victoria. She was a stickler. Punctilious in an annoying way. And she was spoiling my party.

"Oh, well, well. You're a rich girl!" Mr. Johnson said. "Then you can live on the bigger island next to Sam's. And you can join us online, too."

It seems a lot of kids had money tucked away. Apparently we were all rich in some *other* part of the world.

* * *

The meat ice box was beginning to overflow. Mom was still in the habit of grocery shopping for pounds of flesh but the leading carnivore was on a hunger strike. She had to cut back and the neighborhood butcher became concerned. She was his number one customer.

"Hi, Mrs. Swine. Something wrong?" asked Mr. Gonzalez. "You're not buying your meats like you used to."

"Sorry, Jose. Mr. Swine has been on a hunger strike for a week. He's not eating like he used to."

"Really? That's real shocking. Is he sick, maybe?"

"No, I think he's just depressed. He thought he was going

to win a million dollars in the lottery but came up empty. He said he saw a green cow".

"Wow! Green cows are good luck. In El Salvador, when there's a green cow, we buy raffle tickets."

"Do your green cows say, *moo-ney?*"

"Money? No, it says, *di-nee-roo.*"

"Perhaps different kind of cow?"

"Well, our cow speaks Spanish. So maybe it's just in the translation. But our people believe green cows are very lucky. Tell your husband to try again."

"Okay, Jose. Hopefully he'll get his appetite back in a few days. Hasta la pizza!"

Mom came home and told Dad about Mr. Gonzalez. She told him that in El Salvador green cows are very lucky too. But they say *di-nee-roo,* not *moo-ney.*

Dad became more despondent. All the signs seemed to point to a jackpot, but he came up empty handed. Why? Did he lack faith? Will? Courage? Did he not show enough humility? Maybe he was too arrogant before the gods?

Who knows? Maybe all those things. Perhaps he was arrogant. He felt overly entitled. And he also lacked faith and courage. He didn't have the mettle to see through all fifty tickets and squarely face fate mano-a-boar. He gave up at forty-eight because he was too afraid to see what the last two held in store for him. He shouted *"no mas!"* before the fight had ended.

Curiously, the cow in his dream transformed into a mad bull. It punished him night after night. Dad dreamt he was a matador, but he was scared to confront the bull. Every night, the bull gave him the horn on the backside. *Ouch!* Dad woke up in a sweat. He wasn't used to being impaled. He wasn't used to being on the receiving end of big horns.

Dad felt ashamed. He wasn't just a coward, he dreamed like a coward. A chicken. A mouse. He looked at himself in the mirror and began to mutter.

"There is no tomorrow . . . There is no tomorrow . . . There is no tomorrow!"

Aren't they lines from a movie? I wasn't sure. It was before my time.

"Sometimes, you just gotta say, what the *heck!* Sometimes, you just gotta say, what the *HECK!*"

Hmmm . . . that sounded familiar too. Dad seemed to be stealing lines from old films.

"You've gotta ask yourself one question. *Do you feel lucky?* Well, do ya, punk? Do *you* feel lucky? Do ya?!"

Yeah, that's from Dirty Harry. I know that one by heart.

Dad was psyching himself up for something. I don't know what. Maybe he was going to take it to the bull. Grow some cojones and be a matador. Lord god Shiva, destroyer of worlds. Powerful impaler. Bloodcurdling carnivore. Terrifying, savage beast. King of the jungle. Mighty warthog of the dry savannas.

* * *

I had left Dad's two remaining tickets on the coffee table. I didn't bother to scratch. Dad had given up on them, and I assumed they were losers too.

Dad barreled into the living room screaming. "If you want a guarantee, buy a toaster!" Dad didn't buy an appliance. He was cavorting with dreams. Dancing with Lucy Luck. Tugging on a line to the moon. He took a chance with lottery tickets and he was determined to see it through. No guarantees. Just face the consequences of his silly gamble or the best decision of his life. "Life's a box of chocolates!" he hollered

Dad grabbed the first lottery ticket and began to scratch. His beady eyes became as sharp as his determination.

Loser. *No soup for you!*

"There's no crying in baseball!" he shouted.

Dad almost keeled over but remained undeterred. He was going to face his demons. Mom was enjoying the spectacle. She was sitting at the edge of her seat. Her mouth was stuffed with popcorn.

"I can handle the truth!" Dad yelled. "After all, tomorrow is another day!"

He gathered himself, squinted his eyes even tighter and slowly began to scratch. Scratch. Scratch . . .

CONTRATULATION! YOU HAVE WON $100,000.

"Woohooo!" Dad screamed. "Today, I consider myself the luckiest man on the face of the earth! As God is my witness, I'll never be hungry again!" Dad jumped and hooted like a crazy boar.

The movie quotes were giving me vertigo. Mom capsized and choked on her popcorn. I tried to help her back up but she felt like the sinking Titanic. I got her a glass of icy water and she was fortunately okay.

"Show me the money! Show me the money! I'm the king

of the world! I'm the king of the world!"

I wonder if it's true what they say. *Life is a banquet, and most poor suckers are starving to death.* Maybe too many of us rely on the kindness of strangers. And if that disappoints, we're left with nothing, not even our own two clay feet.

When Mom cleared her throat, she let out a loud oink. The neighborhood dogs howled on cue. It was a symphony of noise and commotion. Everyone seemed to be celebrating.

Regardless of setbacks, we probably shouldn't let it stop us or we could end up like Dad grazing on dandelions. In the face of disappointment, don't be discouraged. Indeed, expect setbacks and disappointments. And if it comes, do something about it.

Least of all, throw in the towel. Instead, find another stranger to lend a helping hand. Make her an offer she can't refuse. There's more than one sow in the disco. Or support yourself on stilts until you get your legs back. But don't give up unless it's your *choice* to walk away. No regrets. No excuses in the back of your head that it might have been if only for *so and so.* That's poison.

* * *

Dad was back to his old self except a little richer. The house was very noisy again. The meat storage freezer was close to empty and Mom was busy at Mr. Gonzalez's butcher shop. Jose smiled at her and said, "I told you so!" He was glad because his favorite customer was back and business was booming.

I hadn't decided what I'm going to do with my hundred dollars. After doing some research, it turns out it's not very much. Back in 1950, it would be worth less than ten dollars. How can money be worth less? Isn't it supposed to go up in value? Whoever is in charge should be fired!

Dad also stopped dreaming of bulls. It was back to arguing with imaginary strangers and old friends who still owed him money. I could hear him mumbling and yelling at 3:05 a.m. in the morning. Cows would appear sometimes, but they were the black and white kind. And usually as steak on a platter, medium rare.

Dad's lottery win wouldn't make him a rich man here or frankly anywhere, but it would serve as a nice addition to the Swine family rainy day fund. The victory was also more moral than financial. Dad confronted his fears, regardless of consequences, and that in itself was something to cheer. After all, he could have just as well lost as well as win. But whatever comes, face it like a pig. Few things are guaranteed. Green cows or not, a dream is just a dream. But if it says *moo-ney*, you might want to buy some lottery tickets.

6

PIG STY

"This isn't yoga! Yoga is fresh and clean!"

My mom is probably the biggest pig in the world. I don't mean just her weight or girth, though they're pretty massive, even Dad concedes. But figuratively, too. She's neither the maid type. Nor the showering type. Nor much of anything related to cleaning *up*, throwing *out*, wiping *down*, or keeping things organized and in their place type. She does love to eat, which is an *in* activity and disappearing act of its own kind, I suppose. But it doesn't address the problem of personal odor, dusty tables, general clutter, disarray, and nose-high piles of laundry.

Of course, Mom vehemently denies any of this and feels insulted at even the thought that she fails to take care of herself or the house. After all, she's a lady from England of very high breeding. She's certified one hundred percent British Lop and not a droplet of admixture. A mutt or mongrel she is not. She even has papers to prove it. In a different time, she would be wearing a first place ribbon and paraded around like a beauty queen. It's only recent norms and standards that expect something leaner, tidier, and domestic from her. It's not very fair, she argues. After all, she was bred to be this way.

Dad mostly agrees, although I'm not sure whether that's due to his conjugal obligations or genuine honesty. But maybe she has a point, too. British Lops are pretty massive the same way Scandinavians are blonde and sumo wrestlers are swarthy. But how do we explain her aversion to bath water and vacuum cleaners? Surely, there's nothing hereditary about that. Curiously, she enjoys mud treatments and saunas. She could roll around in watery pools of soft sand for hours.

"Nothing better to beat the heat," she says, grinning from ear to ear. "Or the cold. Mud keeps you warm in the winter and cool in summer!"

Did Mom inadvertently discover the solution to climate change? No more air conditioning or central heating. Just water, silt, and bodies covered in black mud. Pig pens will one day become the norm like indoor plumbing.

* * *

It's not easy finding stuff around the house. Everything is disorganized. There's no single place for pans, can openers, paper towels, and forks. Things are randomly everywhere and that's where it's exactly supposed to be, Mom alleges. But as far as I can tell, it's there for no particular reason except it just happens to be left there. The kitchen drawers, for instance, are filled with a hundred different random items based on no apparent logic. It's a farrago.

The floors are also a mess. Grocery bags float on the ground like dense plastic fog. Sacks of onions, potatoes, and carrots sit tenuously in the middle of the living room awaiting permanent locations. Kitchen appliances randomly appear on the floor like traveling vagabonds. If you don't watch your step, you're likely to step on something or bump into it.

"Mom, you have to be better organized!" I complain. "Spoons should go with other utensils. Cleaning sprays should go with other cleaning products. There should be some rational order to where you put things."

"Everything is where it's supposed to be, dear," Mom says. "Let's not be too rear end. If you don't like plastic bags on the floor, don't just kick it away! Move them to the storage bin in the garage. You have two hands!"

Dad doesn't seem to mind too much. Maybe he's grown accustomed to the chaotic potpourri and inured to the shambolic arrangement. Or has he always been this way? A partner in crime. An enabler.

"Wouldn't it be nice to vacuum the house?" I once asked.

"Sure would! There's a reason I don't live in the forest on dirt floor."

"Then maybe you should tell Mom to clean the house? And pick things up after herself."

"It's complicated, son. Tell a woman what to do and you

could get yourself into a mound of trouble. Sometimes, you've got to go with the flow. Pick your battles. It's like playing the lottery. You've got to know when to pay. And when to hold onto your wallet."

For most twelve-year-olds, a mother's penchant for clutter and lack of personal hygiene can work to his advantage. When Dad yells that I should clean up my room or take a bath before bed, she gives me convenient cover.

"What about Mom! She never does!" I say. "And have you seen the house? It's a pig sty."

"Don't talk about your mom or house like that!" Dad reprimands sternly.

Perhaps I shouldn't, but it's true.

Mom has an indoor mud pen in her room and she loves to roll around in it. Sometimes she gets up and walks to the kitchen leaving mud tracks. It's enough to make even a messy kid go ballistic.

"Mom! You're leaving mud all over the kitchen!" I yell at her.

"It's just a little dirt. It won't kill you," she casually retorts. "Don't be so uptight."

Dad binge cleans sometimes. And I hear him complain, too, mumbling to himself. "I won the lottery . . . people think I'm rich. Wealthy people don't live like this . . ."

Sometimes he tells Mom that she could be a better homemaker. But little surprise, it makes her quite upset. She'll sulk in her mud bath and mutter to herself. "He has two hoofs! He can clean just as well as I can. Why do I have to do everything?"

I admit that it's embarrassing when guests come over. My

friends wonder whether it's a house or animal farm. They've gotten lost between my room and the kitchen when they have to make the journey for milk and soda. Piles of laundry stacked on top of one another can resemble ominous, maze-like, mountain ranges.

When they find their way back to my room, Mom's panties are hanging from their heads and dirty socks are wrapped around their necks like nooses. They tell me they thought they were going to die. They show me foot injuries from toaster booby traps and twenty pounds of frozen turkey wandering the floor.

* * *

Habits can be some of the hardest things to change. According to my math teacher, Mr. McCoy, habits are like formulas stuck in our heads. We do the same math over and over again and can't stop the subroutine.

My history teacher, Mr. Johnson, compares habits to the fate of history. We can try to change the future but the past has often predetermined tomorrow like letters etched in stone.

But Ms. Jones, my health teacher, says habits can be changed in as little as twenty-two minutes. It just takes a shift in the way we think. She says that when she does yoga the world can suddenly flip upside down. And that's not just because she's standing on her head.

"Hiya, Sam! How's it going?" Mr. Johnson greeted me

before third period history class.

"Good morning, Mr. Johnson. I'm fine," I said.

"You know there's a woman's underpants stuck to your back pocket? Is that a new look?" he asked wryly. "I see you like granny panties."

"Uh oh! No . . . It's my mom's. She's so untidy," I confessed. "She leaves piles of her clothes everywhere and it ends up in my pocket. Inside my shirt. Or my ears."

"Wow!" gasped Mr. Johnson, sitting back in his easy chair, twisting his long mustache. "My dog used to go into the laundry room and run around in Mrs. Johnson's bra wrapped around its head. Sometimes he ran to the neighbor's house and delivered it as a gift to Mr. Walkowski. He started to believe it was a secret message from my wife."

Huh? I looked at him blankly. I was too young to comprehend the devious artifice of grown up infidelity.

"Mr. Walkowski is divorced," Mr. Johnson explained. "After those embarrassing episodes, the laundry room was locked up away from Fido. But I had told her a hundred times about keeping the laundry room closed. She never listened to me."

"Maybe women don't like to take advice from men?" I mused.

"Haha! And the converse, too, my boy! Habits are difficult to change but sometimes mortification, like revolution, can move the historical needle!" he said with a big hearty laugh.

I don't know if he was serious, but maybe it's true? Maybe Mom could be goaded into a new future world through ignominy and humiliation? Mom could be pretty shameless but public embarrassment was one of her weak spots.

* * *

When I came home, I found Mom's smelly bra in a mountain pile and wore it like a hat and ran around the house like a crazy boy raised by wolves. Unfortunately, no effect. Mom looked at me dumbfounded and asked insouciantly, "are you growing boobs on your head?"

So much for that.

Next, I pretended to slip on muddy tracks and plastic bags left behind by you-know-who and fall over a pile of her old clothes, sprain my ankle, and break my neck on an electric blender on the floor. I screamed like a four-year-old preschooler in horrible pain.

But Mom yelled over my faux cries that I should watch where I'm going. She said she had her clothes nicely stacked for the laundry. She told me to stop bawling like a three-year-old baby.

Somehow, this didn't seem to be working.

As a reserved English pig, Mom hates exposing the family laundry to the public. So for my third try, I thought I'd expose her dirty underwear to the public. Literally.

However, as an introverted scion of a British sow who avoids public embarrassment, the chromosome for humiliation didn't pass over my generation. I was probably as vulnerable to feelings of social discomfort as she was. Did I really want to be caught up as collateral damage? I could only hope it will embarrass Mom more than it will me.

When she was in the backyard watering her petunias, I hurriedly gathered her personal belongings and hauled them to the front lawn. I threw her underpants here. Her smelly brassiere there. Her undershirts were catapulted into the street. Her socks perambulated to the neighbors. And her stockings hung from lampposts like convicted medieval felons.

I thought I was successful on the sly when I bumped into Dad on my way back to the house. *Uh oh.* He rolled his eyes and seemed more exasperated than angry. When I turned around to retreat the other way, I noticed a small gathering of neighbors gawking at the scene. My public humiliation was complete.

"Watcha doin', Sam!" Mr. Walton, the neighbor across the street, asked archly. He's an insurance salesman and likes to spread neighborhood *news* on his email newsletter. He sold Dad our home and car insurance policies. This is not the guy I want to be seeing.

"Nothing, Mr. Walton. Just hanging . . . laundry." My face had turned fire truck red.

"Haha! Do you only do women's underpants? Or men's, too? You might want to go easy on the starch," Mr. Walton said. "Lots of holes! Premiums are higher on holy artifacts!" The crowd erupted in laughter.

Dad waved the neighbors off and we silently gathered Mom's clothes from the street. But trying to reclaim stockings hanging from lampposts was a little tricky.

I was grounded for a month and my last attempt to transmute shame into a bright new future turned out to be a debacle. Meanwhile, Mom was no more the wiser. She hadn't a clue that her brassiere was supine on the lawn and the neighbors know that her undergarments are as holey as they are shades of amber.

* * *

The next day I walked into English class more sullen than usual. My English teacher, Ms. Fearstein, was probably the most hated teacher in school. Students feared and toadied up to her in equal measure. Except me. It was just dread.

Ms. Fearstein was an old lady that was smaller than most girls in the seventh grade, but she's allegedly survived wars, famines, plagues, hurricanes, typhoons, tsunamis, tornadoes, floods, earthquakes, avalanches, giant sinkholes, and riots. Or so her story goes. And nothing scares her, she claims, though she seems more paranoid than anyone I've ever known.

I think I saw fear in her eyes when she was attacked by a grasshopper. It jumped on her head and crawled underneath her wig. She screamed that the grasshopper was drilling holes into her brain. The school nurse finally persuaded her to remove her wig and the grasshopper jumped out. One of the girls in class stepped on it. She should have stomped on the wig. I think it was moving.

Ms. Fearstein would go on to tell the story of the grasshopper as a swarm of locusts that invaded the classroom. In her overwrought mind, it was a plague of pharaonic proportions.

"Why the grim face?" asked Laura. She sat to my right and spoke three languages fluently. "You seem more depressed than usual."

"I am," I confessed. I was just trying to keep up with one. "Public humiliation and a month of grounding don't add to a kid's happiness."

"What happened? What did you get caught doing?" Laura was a blonde from Columbia with a moderate overbite. Dad says I should be nice to her because when she gets that fixed, she's going to be a beaut.

"It's too embarrassing to talk about. Let's say I exposed the family's dirty laundry."

"Who gave you permission to talk?" barked Ms. Fearstein. "This is Honors English, not Mr. Wu's Dry Cleaning!"

"Sorry, Ms. Fearstein," Laura said meekly, turning to face the front of the class.

"Who's Mr. Wu?" I asked.

"You're Mr. Wu! At least based on what's going around the grapevine!" Ms. Fearstein said scornfully. "Do you have room for my laundry? But easy on the starch, kiddo!"

Good grief . . .

In history class, Mr. Johnson wondered how things were going at home. He said embarrassment was only as humiliating as my desire to keep up appearances. I didn't really understand but it was supposed to be replete with profundity.

"How's the home life?" Mr. Johnson asked.

"Not too good," I said glumly. "Mom is still a pig. Embarrassment doesn't seem to faze her. I walk around with her underwear on my head and she asks whether extra pairs of boobs are growing on my head. And I just embarrassed myself in front of the world."

"Haha!" laughed Mr. Johnson. "Maybe your mom doesn't respond well to criticism."

"It seems so . . ."

"Well, it's not the end of the world. In about five years, you'll be off to college. And there will be a heap of new embarrassments to feel humiliated about."

"That's good to know," I said as the bell rang, signaling the start of class.

In nutrition class, Ms. Jones suggested that I might want to try mindful breathing to alleviate stress. Anxiety isn't good for a kid, she reminded me. My skin could break out. I could develop a tick. Maybe Tourette's syndrome. I might say things uncontrollably I don't want to say.

"Take it easy on your mom," admonished Ms. Jones. "She's only human."

"Actually, she's a pig," I said.

"Yes, she's a pig. Messy like a pig. But she's your mom."

"She hardly showers. And the house is a pig sty."

"I hear ya, Sam. I personally like to keep a clean house and body myself. But sometimes, you just have to go with the flow. Accept things as they are, not as you want them to be. Wanting can be a source of great suffering."

"That's what my dad said."

"He probably has the right idea. Some people can change in twenty-two minutes. Some people need twenty-two years."

"In twenty-two years I'll be an old man!"

"Actually, you'll still be young. I'm almost twenty-two years older than you are . . ."

"Really? That old?! Wow! Sorry."

I decided to take Ms. Jones' word to heart and ease up. So what if Mom was a pig? And the house was dirty? And the floor was littered with grocery bags that resembled petroleum fog? I'm a kid. I'm flexible. Adaptable. Pliable. I can eat anything without getting indigestion or heartburn. I can do five thousand sit-ups without getting tired. I can run for miles before collapsing. I can watch TV up close or afar. I have perfect eyesight. My brain is like a sponge. I absorb everything. I'm a human machine. And I can be as swine as my mom!

* * *

It's funny how adaptable humans are. I stopped bathing and while it bothered me at first, I gradually got used to the feeling. My hair stopped itching. And my body took comfort in accumulated layers of oil and sweat on the epidermis. Grime formed a natural coating on the skin that protected me from infections and bacteria.

I still brushed my teeth because I didn't want cavities. But I don't think I did much more than that. I wore the same clothes. And my grades even improved because I had so much more time and less stress. Or maybe my teachers felt sorry for me. I tried mindful breathing and I could count to a hundred without forgetting my place. It's remarkable how stress free life can be when you just stop caring. Maybe want is the source of all suffering?

But before long, things began to get really bad. And very nasty. You'd think there's an upper limit to odor. And filth. But there really isn't.

"Yo . . . you stink!" said Danny.

"I know. It's my new *thing*," I said.

"Yeah, but that shouldn't be a *thing!*" he insisted.

"C'mon. Leave him alone," said Scott. "He says that's his new *thing*. We should respect that."

"No, no! We're his best friends. We have to tell him it's not okay!" Danny argued.

"But who says it's not okay? That's just society!" countered Scott. "A hundred years ago, none of us would be bathing and changing clothes."

Ms. Fearstein wasn't too happy with my new *thing,* either. She kicked me out of class and said I should go to school in a stable with other cows and horses.

"You smell worse than shoes!" declared Ms. Fearstein.

"It's just the way I smell," I said. "It might run in the family."

"Maybe he can't afford to shower, Ms. Fearstein," Laura remonstrated in the way of my defense. "You can't discriminate against poor people."

"I sure can! Fetid children belong in barns, not schools."

"Maybe he lacks resources? School should serve as a safe space for all children, regardless of economic situation."

"When I was a kid, we had nothing!" Ms. Fearstein insisted. "No plumbing. We lived in slums. The ghetto. The barrios . . . But we bathed! We sponged!"

"I'll leave," I said.

Mr. McCoy wondered if my new *thing* was an

experimental algorithm or a fixed equation. He let me stay in class but asked me to take a seat next to the window. He cracked a smile and said my funky odor helped him appreciate cats.

Mr. Johnson was more understanding. He chuckled and said I must have really abandoned any pretense of keeping up appearances. He said he sort of admired what I was doing but I should really consider taking a shower and changing my clothes sometime.

Ms. Jones almost keeled over when she took a whiff of me. She didn't realize how bad little boys can smell. I told her that I owed it all to her.

"What do you mean, you owe it all to me?" a confused Ms. Jones demanded. "I didn't say you shouldn't bathe and change your clothes!"

"I know. But you told me to go with the flow. No resistance. No antagonism. No antipathy. Just accept things as they are. You said want leads to suffering."

"Yes . . . I guess I did. I just didn't know it would be this kind of *flow*. I didn't mean you should stop caring. You really stink. And your clothes are filthy. You smell putrid."

"I know. But I fit right in at home. Mom and I have gotten close. And I'm less anxious and stressed out. It's like I'm in a permanent state of yoga."

"This isn't yoga! Yoga is fresh and clean!"

Ms. Jones didn't think this was alright. And she felt responsible. She appeared troubled and concerned. Very *unyoga*. She wrote me a note to take to my parents. She enclosed it in a sealed envelope.

* * *

When I came home, I gave the note to Dad, who read it, and then gave it to Mom. Mom read it, and almost cried. I asked her what was wrong but she wouldn't tell me. I tried to read what the note said but she tore it up and ate it.

She looked at me and noticed how disheveled I was. She looked at herself and saw a resemblance. Except for the girth and snout, we were almost like twins. She almost started to cry again.

Quietly, Mom started to clean around the house. She picked up bags from the floor, and put the potatoes and carrots away. Dad labeled things. CLEANING SUPPLIES. TAPE. PENS/PENCILS. POTS/PANS. EATING UTENSILS. And items around the house started to find permanent homes.

Mom discovered the vacuum in the garage and turned it on. It was a novel experience. The *vroom!* scared her at first. But then she enjoyed the power. The sound of clatter and other awful noise was horrifying to me. It was picking up all sorts of things we hadn't a clue existed.

Going with the flow, I did my part cleaning up my room. I put everything away the best I could, the way it used to be. Maybe wanting wasn't all bad?

The laundry machine was also working overtime. Everything that needed to get washed was getting cleaned and put away. No more leaving dirty laundry out in the living room, Mom said. No more mountain ranges. No more laundry tsunamis.

When the day was gone, Mom took a long, hot bath. When she emerged, she was pink like fresh pork. I didn't remember seeing her that way in a long time.

Dad reluctantly took a shower as well to show he was a team player. The plumbing clogged up. He had to get out his tools and fix it. So much hair. He's a very hairy guy.

* * *

Back in school, people stopped avoiding me. Mr. McCoy said I could return to my regular seat, having removed the noisome variable. Ms. Fearstein let me back in class, though she tried to find other excuses to keep me out.

"You look so handsome today, Sam," said Laura. "New hair cut?"

"Thanks. You're not so bad yourself," I said. "Just a shower."

Danny and Scott each tried to take credit for my rehabilitation. Danny said it was tough love that forced me to clean myself up. He said I was like a drug addict that needed powerful intervention.

Scott said it was compassion and tolerance that finally brought me back to my old self. It's loyal friends like him that remind ne'er-do-wells like me that there's hope in a sometimes seemingly hopeless world of never-ending suffering.

Mr. Johnson guffawed when I told him about Ms. Jones and her note. We were both curious to learn what it said.

But Ms. Jones was mum. She said it was a personal message between women. Women are the foundation of the universe, she believes. They're like the Earth. The very ground we walk on. *She* gives us place, home, and love, Ms. Jones said.

It sounded pretty good, but my head was starting to feel airy.

"I hope you keep up your yoga, Sam!" Ms. Jones said. "It's never too young to start."

"There's a lot of poses to learn. But I get bored easily."

"Overcoming boredom is part of the exercise. You have to learn to be *just* with your thoughts and body. Relaxed but taut. Supple but strong. It's not easy."

"Is that what you told my mom?"

"Not in so many words. But we do have to find *balance* in everything."

7

THE IRASCIBLE NEIGHBOR

"Blood was splattered everywhere. Wokou pirates were screaming Japanese in my head."

D ad thinks we have an irascible neighbor. But coming from him, I can't be sure whether it's the neighbor, Dad or something else. He's not exactly normal himself. Dad screams and yells randomly and the horrible sounds of his booms echo through the neighborhood. Maybe the next door neighbor is having an acoustical mental breakdown.

"He's an out of work engineer, divorced and lives by himself," Dad sneered. "He sleeps during the day and scurries around at night. He could be burying dead bodies."

I'm not exactly sure what he's up to but I hear noises at 11 p.m. waking me up from my amazing dreams only twelve-year-olds can have. I've been going to war with diabolical android robots equipped with super intelligent AI and crossing swords with one-legged pirates. "Aye-eye, matey!" they keep saying to me. "Where's the hidden treasure!" I demand. Sadly, they won't answer. Maybe they don't speak English? They travel the seven seas and bury treasures across six continents. Surely, one or two boxes of gold for a kid won't put a hole in their EBITDA!

"The crazy guy is fouling up our lawn. There's dirt all over the place!" Dad yelled with heaving and exasperation. "His plumbing is leaking so much water it's flooding our side of the property. I should sue him! *Arrgggghhhh! Buuuuurpp!*"

My science teacher, Mrs. Porter, says that the average depth of the ocean is 2.65 miles. That doesn't seem like a lot. I would have guessed at least a thousand miles.

The ocean covers over seventy percent of the earth. Maybe our property will flood and conjoin with the seven seas? Our front yard could be a beach. I'll become a Barbary pirate.

"Honey, you mustn't upset yourself," Mom implored. "Just try calmly talking to Mr. Green. Maybe you can offer to fix it for him?"

"I tried talking to him a few days ago and he ignored me. He's a very irritable guy. He sped away in his thirty year old jalopy and blew smoke in my face. And I don't work for free! A man should be paid for honest work."

"That's rude . . ." Mom said, reflecting to herself. "Maybe you said something to upset him?"

"No, I didn't! *ARRHHGGGHHHHHH!*" Dad hollered.

"Bbbbuuurrp." He tromped away, retreating outside to simmer.

* * *

Minutes later the sound of hollering battered the kitchen. It was Dad. It seems he had accosted the neighbor and was ready to chop heads.

"You're destroying my lawn! That's destruction of personal property!" Dad roared.

"Sorry, Mr. Swine . . . I have a *(garbled)* plumbing. I told you. I'm trying to *(garbled)* but don't have the *(garbled)* now."

Mr. Green sounded pretty meek for an irascible murderer.

"You're an engineer. You should know how to fix these things!" Dad argued.

"Not quite an engineer—"

"You have a PhD!"

"Yes, true, but—"

"Argghh! Incompetent!" Dad snarled, storming off back into the house with mud up to his ankles. "I can't believe that guy!" Dad shouted, standing in the living room, soiling the floor.

"Honey, you're upsetting yourself too much," Mom said. "Maybe you should just fix it for him. And you're leaving mud tracks in the kitchen."

"I'm not fixing things for free. The guy is broke!"

"Yes, so maybe that's why you should fix it for him. He can pay you back when he has money."

"Cash on the barrel! No credit! I've been ripped off too many times by bums like him!"

"But you'd be helping yourself, too," Mom said, trying to insert some modicum of reason to chaotic emotions.

"I'd rather be knee deep in water than help him. His immigrant wife once insulted me! She called me a loudmouth something . . ."

"Oh dear . . . some foreigners can be quite blunt, can't they?" Mom said. "But she's right. You are loud! What's her name, again? Nenita? She was a waif of a thing. Wasn't she from some tropical island somewhere? I haven't seen in her months. What happened to her?"

"He probably has her buried in the yard, I'm telling you! They used to argue like Mexican Chihuahuas. This used to be quiet neighborhood! *Arrgghhhh!*"

* * *

Mom and I hadn't paid too much attention to the leak in the front yard. As a kid, I didn't really care. And as a mom, she was busy enjoying her mud baths indoors and her gardening in the back. The front was usually the province of Dad's concern. He loved his beautiful, green lawn.

Later that evening, Mom and I went out to examine the damage. A quarter of the front lawn had turned into a lagoon of muddy water. Mom's eyes seemed to light up. Did she want to jump in? Her comportment belied the temptation roiling within.

"Oh . . . what a mess!" Mom said, trying to disguise her secrets.

Maybe the pool of water would get bigger and become a future habitat for frogs? And eventually alligators.

"I kinda like it. It could be our front yard pool," I said.

"Our beautiful green lawn is so muddy and dirty. Your father spends so much time taking care of it. And all this water. What a waste . . ."

"Hey, why don't you roll around out here, Mom?"

"Don't be silly! What would the neighbors say?"

Mom had some strange personal habits but she was usually self-aware enough to guard them in secrecy. No dirty laundry left out for the neighbors to ogle. She was a pig but a private one. She's British and the Brits have their pride and assiduously mind their public manners.

* * *

I was in a veritable battle zone of fog, smoke, and rain. Pirates and AI robots were everywhere. One-eyed ocean marauders tried to slice my limbs and disembowel my guts. Why were they so cruel?

I tried to move but the air felt like quicksand. My body was in slow motion. Terrible! I hate it when I'm lethargic and sluggish in my own imagination.

I heard shoveling sounds in the distance. Trenches were being dug. Maybe a grave for me! *Chuugg! Chuugg! Chuugg!* Bombs exploded. Cannon fire. Pyrotechnics over the horizon.

Nearby, desperate bodies were engaged in mortal combat. I want to join in but I have no weapon. Frustrating!

I awoke to the sound of dirt and shovels. It was the irascible neighbor again. What was he doing? I wasn't sure whether I should thank him for saving me or resent him for waking me. It was 11:37 p.m. I have school tomorrow. Kids need their sleep before a long day of misery.

I peeked out the window and saw him working. Digging. Why? Was he really burying dead bodies? Large gray bags. Crimson colored water. Is that blood? Uh oh. Through bleary eyes, it all looked red. The walls seemed to be marinated in pungent tomato sauce. The lights were like ruby. Blood was splattered everywhere. I was three-quarters asleep. Wokou pirates were screaming Japanese in my head.

I withdrew back to bed and concealed my body under the blanket. It was a special blanket only possessed by prepubescent boys to protect them from danger. I had heard of butchers slaughtering pigs by the thousands in giant warehouses in the Midwest. I never thought it would happen in my neighborhood. My parents together could feed at least half the town of Suidae Valley. Starvation could be eliminated in the West Coast. Pork would replace chicken as the most popular white meat. My parents could be in danger. *Sigh.* This was terrible. A swarm of robotic cyclops stormed the battlefield. *Where is my laser gun?!*

* * *

The next morning I groggily awoke to the sound of Dad unceremoniously burping through the hallway and grunting down the stairs. I brushed my teeth, combed my hair, and dressed for school. I wasn't looking forward to school. The call of sleep beckoned like chocolate cake at a birthday party. Cake was especially solicitous this morning.

I waited for the bus just outside my house. My stomach was gurgling with milk and cereal. The latent alligator pond sat over my shoulders. Then Mr. Green emerged from his house. He smiled at me. I think. Was it me? I looked around. There was no one else here. He then gestured with his hand for me to approach. Why? He might be a pig murderer. Holodomor. Holocaust. I'm not a pig but I'm related to some. Dutifully, I trundled over to Mr. Green.

"Hiya, Sam. How are you?"

He looked more disheveled up close. His hair was growing like crabgrass weeds and his chin was bushier than his head. I'd guess he was in his early sixties but he was hunched over like a centenarian. Altercations with Dad can do that.

"Good . . . Mr. Green . . . Uh . . . What can I do for you?"

"Oh, glad you asked. You see, my car wouldn't start this morning. And I need to get to the post office to pick up a package. I was wondering if you wouldn't mind doing that for me? The post office is right next to your school, isn't it?"

"Yes, it is." Dang it! Why did I tell him that?

"Would you mind? There's an extra ten dollars here for your trouble. Get yourself a hamburger!"

Hamburger? Ham? *Pork?* Diabolical!

"Oh . . . no, I don't mind. I'd be happy to pick up your package for you, sir."

"Good, good . . . Here's a signed note for you to present to the lady at the post office. I'll call them to let them know you'll be coming over later to pick up a package for me."

"Okay." I smiled but I was kicking myself underneath.

HONK! HONK!

"Oh! Your bus is here! You'd better get going. See you later this afternoon, Sam. And thanks again!"

I read Mr. Green's note. It wasn't anything special. PLEASE GIVE MY PACKAGE TO SAM. HE'S SWINE, BUT A VERY NICE BOY. THANK YOU. MR. GREEN. And then signed with his home address and phone number.

"What's that you have, Sam!" one of the boys in the bus yelled out. His name was Johnny and he had a paunch. It must run in the family because his dad also has a paunch.

"Nothing. Just a note for the post office."

"I heard the old man is a killer! He's burying dead bodies!" another boy exclaimed. It was Steve and his red hair seemed to dance on his head like wild tribal fire. He should really try to comb his hair sometimes. He can be such a pig.

"Where did you hear that?" I asked incredulously.

"From my dad . . . who heard it from *your* dad!" he answered.

Good grief. My dad was spreading rumors everywhere. What a loudmouth. He talks to everyone in the neighborhood and everyone can hear every word whether they want to or not! His voice booms through the troposphere like megaphones.

"I don't know if he's a killer. But I heard him last night

digging—"

"*Gasp!* Then it's true!" the kids screamed in chorus.

"I don't know! Let's not jump to conclusions. I just have to pick up a package for him—"

"We should open the package and check for body parts!" Steve said. He was so excited his head bobbed up and down like a bobblehead.

"We can alert the police if we find anything suspicious," Johnny added.

"That's unlawful!" a voice interjected. It was Victoria. She wore glasses almost as thick as Johnny's midsection. "It's a felony to open someone else's mail."

"Oh, be quiet!" Johnny said.

"We're just kids. They can't arrest us," Steve yelped.

"Your parents could be arrested and they'll take you away. You'll live with foster parents until you're adults," Victoria warned.

"You're making that up!" Johnny shot back. "You read too many dystopian books."

"Hunger Games is real!"

Meantime, while the other kids argued about the plausibility of a miserable future, I slunk into my seat trying to make myself disappear . . .

* * *

School can be grueling. Today was one of those days. I didn't get enough sleep. Usually, you look forward to the end of torture, but I wasn't looking forward to the end of school. I would have to make the painful trek to the the post office across the street and then catch the school bus. The kids would probably be curious and demand answers. But did we want to know? Can we handle the truth?

Johnny and the gang had spread news about the "killer's package." Some children got overly excited and cried into their milks. Mommies were called. Parents demanded safe spaces for their kids. Some asked about my ethnic background. Was I Russian? Muslim? Chinese? *Swine* was not a traditional American name, they said. Teachers tried to assuage fears. Some tried to get confirmation. "So, Sam, where . . . are you from, exactly?"

"Right here, Mrs. Lopez. I was born here in Suidae Valley!" But that didn't seem to satisfy them. There were whispers about a DNA test. Parents demanded copies of my birth certificate. Some speculated I was born in Kenya. 32andMe rejected my swab sample. They said it was *suid*. Of course it's Suid!

I wasn't sure whether I should inspect the package or not. Scott said all professionals, like his dentist father, have a fiduciary duty. Danny said a delivery person just delivers. It's not his job to check the contents. They both had a point. But was I just a delivery man or professional? I was getting paid. And I was making a delivery. I was part of the *gig* economy. I was confused.

When the bell rang at the end of the last period, I walked over to the post office in the white brick building across the street. My math teacher, Mr. McCoy, said that the post office was going bankrupt. Their numbers were in the red. It didn't add up. But there didn't seem to be any shortage of customers. The line was long. The postal workers at the counter were chatty and worked at a leisurely pace.

Fortunately, a rotund woman who resembled Mom from behind let me in front of her. She said her dog was about my age. She asked if I enjoyed walks. Since I was here to just pick up a package, most people didn't seem to mind my intrusion. It shouldn't take long, the postal employee said. They just had to go to the back and find it.

When the man came back, I signed for the large yellow package and began to make my way out. A bald man in a black suit glared at me and gave me the thumbs down sign. A skinny woman with short hair stared and followed me with her evil eye. She had been waiting forty minutes. When I neared the exit door she pointed her long finger at me, and seemed to say, "You're going to get it!" She scared me. I didn't mean to jump the line. Someone let me cut in. What's a kid supposed to do? Turn down the offer?

Traumatized slightly, I started my way back to school. The package itself looked innocuous. The weight felt innocuous. I shook it and it didn't explode. It seemed there was just paper inside. Maybe Mr. Green wasn't a pig Holodomor after all?

I spotted my friends in the distance, and Danny and Scott ran to meet me.

"You got it, huh?" Scott said. "Can I see?"

"Uh . . . I don't know . . . I guess."

"Only the delivery man should handle the package," Danny reminded.

Scott took a look, saw nothing unusual, and handed it

back to me. "Feels like documents inside, the kind my dad always gets from insurance companies."

He was almost right. The sender was a law office. Divorce lawyer.

"I just remembered. Mr. Green gave me ten bucks. Let's get burgers and fries!" I said. "I'm buying!" I was feeling rich and generous.

"Yeah!" the guys cheered.

We had plenty of time for burgers and sodas before the school bus came to collect the kids. But not quite enough money for three hamburgers. However, Scott had three dollars and Danny had a buck. They chipped in making it enough for three hamburgers, sodas, and couple of fries to share. We were happy.

* * *

The ride home was uneventful. A package from a law office could mean almost anything, but probably not body parts. Johnny theorized that it could be spy documents. Steve said it could be anthrax powder. Victoria told everyone to shut up. She was trying to do her homework.

When the bus dropped me off, I went home and put my book bag away. Mom was in her room mud bathing, again. "Dinner will be ready soon, dear!" she shouted. I told her I had eaten already. I wouldn't be hungry again for two more hours. Dad was in the backyard inspecting his grain silo. *I should run over to Mr. Green's house before Dad finds out,* I thought.

I knocked on his door and Mr. Green belatedly answered. He greeted me with a big smile. "Did you get it?" he asked earnestly. He still looked disheveled. Maybe he was taking a nap. His eyes looked crusty and his body appeared to be unaccustomed to being upright.

"Yes, Mr. Green. I have your package."

"Were there any problems?"

"No, sir. The post office was busy but a nice lady let me cut in line."

"Sit down. Let me get you some milk. You want some milk? And some cookies. I have such terrible manners . . ."

"Ummm . . . okay. Are you in trouble or something, Mr. Green?" I probably shouldn't have asked, but it just came out of me. "Sorry. I couldn't help notice the package came from a law office."

Mr. Green fumbled in the kitchen and found a glass. Some milk. And some girl scout cookies.

"No, I'm not in trouble. Not anymore. This is my redemption."

"Your redemption? Are you dying?"

"It felt like that for a while. There should be a check in the package for forty-thousand. And official papers settling my divorce. It's finally all over!"

He brought over cookies and milk to the table. I took a bite. They were stale but tasty. Peanut butter chocolate chip. I was full of hamburgers and fries, but there's always extra room for cookies.

"I guess you don't know. But my wife left me about six months ago and her lawyers froze my bank account. They demanded a lot of money from me. Too much."

"Wow . . . wasn't she from the islands? I don't think she liked my dad much."

"Well, your father . . . he can be difficult. Stubborn and hot headed. Pardon me. I shouldn't say that about your father."

Mr. Green carefully opened his package to inspect its contents. And sure enough, there was a check for forty-thousand. A big smile of relief appeared across his face. Then he read a letter entitled, FINAL DIVORCE SETTLEMENT.

Mr. Green's bank account would be unfrozen and his pension reinstated. His wife had attempted to claim much of his personal assets. She got a goodly portion but less than she demanded. With her half of the money and alimony, she moved to San Francisco and began attending hair dressing school. Her new boyfriend was half Mr. Green's age.

"My wife is from the islands of Panay. Our age difference, as you might have guessed, is quite significant. But after several years together, it didn't work out. We argued a lot. She's a young woman . . ."

"Sorry to hear that, Mr. Green. We could also hear your arguing from our house. Why did you marry a woman from far away? You don't like *Suidish* girls?"

"Yes. And I can overhear your father all the time, too! Oh, the sounds he makes! But that's okay, he's a warthog. I know."

He looked away, gazing into the space of his past. His eyes seemed to glisten. His mouth quivered slightly.

"It's not so easy for a man like me to find a woman here," he said. "Women are not easy. You'll find out someday,

Sam."

I was just twelve and didn't quite understand modern gender dysfunction. But I felt sorry for men like Mr. Green. He shopped for a woman halfway across the world. And still, she left him with half his money for another man half his age.

"She was immature. But I hoped we could make it work," he continued. "But she became so demanding. New clothes. Jewelry. Vacations. Expensive restaurants. It bankrupted me. You know, I'm not a rich man. I'm just a botanist. I have a very modest pension."

"What's a botanist?" I asked.

"A botanist studies plants. Your father says I'm an engineer, but I'm actually a trained scientist in plant biology."

"Is that why you work at nights and dig in the ground?"

"Yes. I hope I haven't been disturbing you. I try to be quiet."

"Ummm . . . No."

"I'm working on a new breed of special plants. They need very special care. And special copper heavy plant food. That's what gives it the red color. They can also be sensitive to too much sunlight."

"Ahhh . . ." I said. No buried bodies or blood after all. Just plants. And plant food. Maybe giant *carnivorous plants?*

"Now that I have money, I'm going to fix the leaky water and pay your father for his lawn. I've been trying to explain to him, you know. But he's not easy to talk to when he's upset. He's a plumber, right? I'd like to hire him if he's willing to do the job. So many repairs around the house to make! Now I can pay for it."

Mr. Green appeared almost jovial. It seems he was finally

getting his life back. It's funny how life can turn on a dime. Or rather, a big check.

* * *

I came home and told Dad about Mr. Green's proposal. Dad was surly and demanded "cash on the barrel!" By the following day, the two worked out an agreement. Mr. Green offered generous compensation for Dad's plumbing services and cold, green cash. They also agreed to a landscaper who could fix both their lawns.

Mom was a little sorry to see the muddy pool of water go, however. She secretly dreamed of jumping in. It would have been like old times when she was a little piglet frolicking on the farm. Memories of mud, cool waters, and the warm embrace of the sun in bygone days of youth made up some of the happiest days of her life.

8

STREET FIGHTER

"Bopp. Bopp. Bopp. I'm a machine gun."

When you're not a professional fighter, everything seems to move in slow motion. You can see the punches coming at you, but there's not much you can do because your body is also trapped in the slow motion time warp. *Bopp!* Just as expected. Right in the eye. That's going to be black and blue tomorrow.

It's days like this I wish I had eaten a full breakfast. Of all days, why did I skip breakfast today? I should have been like my dad and said, "Yes!" to scrambled eggs. "Por favor!" to refried frijoles. "More dipping sauce, please!" to cold chicken nuggets. And "encore!" to leftover meatloaf. Instead, it was, "I'm late, Mom. Can't eat. Not hungry, anyway. Just orange juice, please!" Good luck trying to defend yourself on a stomach full of citrus water.

I'm hungry. It's funny feeling hungry in the middle of a fight. I sure could use the energy. Would someone give me a glass of milk? My mouth is so dry.

*　*　*

The boy was on top of me now. An indignant face was looking down with un-boyish grit and anger. What did I do? All I said was that "Joey was like that to everyone." I didn't even see the first punch coming. I wasn't sure it was a *real fight* until he hit me three times. The third punch on the nose finally convinced me those weren't accidents. I'm not just imagining this.

He had mounted me like a mixed martial artist but I'm not sure whether I had pulled guard. How do you do that? It felt like he was sitting on my chest. For sure, I was losing this round. Where are my coaches? I could use some advice.

If there were rounds, my corner men could sit me down and feed me. But this is old school fighting. No breaks. You keep going until someone screams *uncle*. I think I have relatives in Texas, but I don't plan on calling. If there was a referee, he might be looking out for a tap or stoppage. I'm not a tapper but I almost wish someone would throw in the towel.

*　*　*

Nathan was a prickly kid. He didn't go purposely looking for altercations, but he never let an opportunity go to waste. Provocations, insults, and minor slights were fighting words. He was arguably a little troubled. A tough kid. He lived in Danny's neighborhood in one of the beat up apartments. His mom worked for the city. I'm not sure if he had a Dad. Or he traveled a lot. Nathan was held behind a year. He was bigger than most of the other children. Danny almost had a run-in with Nathan but escaped with only wounded pride and public embarrassment. I wish I could escape but I'm not sure I want to in exchange for humiliation and a contused ego. I have to salvage something here. I'm the fastest runner in school but my strength is something to be desired. Why hasn't puberty kicked in yet?

I'm not sure I'm looking forward to growing up. We learned about it in health class. My teacher, Ms. Jones, said it's a beautiful thing. The world opens up. Boys and girls learn to get along, even hold hands. And go out together voluntarily. It's not something I'm looking forward to. I sort of like the division of the sexes. Keeps the world simple. Who says dualism is bad?

In some cultures, men and women are kept separated. Maybe they've realized that puberty isn't all it's cut out to be. You have to shave and use deodorant. Adulthood is high maintenance. You grow hair in places you really shouldn't. It's weird.

Mom says she gained one hundred pounds when she started growing up. People began to look at her and lick their lips. Dad says he gained two hundred pounds of muscle. I'm not sure I want to be that big. Hairy. And girthy. What if I start growing tusks? Do girls like tusks? I wish I was stronger.

* * *

I was trying to fend him off with my hands. I tried to push him away. Or punch his chest. I didn't want to punch his face. I didn't want to be mean. Misdirected compassion. Nathan was stronger and grabbed my wrists. Then he socked me on the head. I think he watches MMA because he tried to elbow me too. Unnecessary roughness. Or maybe he was tired and his elbow needed a place to rest. I'm not sure if they landed or not. I couldn't feel a thing. I was preoccupied with an overgrown kid sitting on my sternum and an audience.

The din of children around me was both loud and silent. Is that possible? There were gawkers, looky-loos, instigators, kibitzers, and provocateurs. "Hit him again!" a kid shouted. "You busted him up good," observed another. "Sam's about to cry!" came a mendacious voice. Liar. Why were they saying those things? I wasn't going to cry. I think. Did they hate me? Kids can be cruel. Adults think children are cute and cuddly. They're not. They forget what they were like when they used to be young. The other kids seemed scared and appalled. They were too afraid to intervene, helpless, and too mesmerized to run. It's funny how you notice these things.

Laura looked as if she might cry. Victoria seemed bored and detached. Probably just passing by on her way to the library. She spends a lot of time at the library. I could see

Danny and Scott to the corner. They were frozen. Uncertain. Should they jump in? Or was that against the rules? Just mano a mano, may the best man win, as the saying goes? No one really knew the rules. We never discussed it. It was never taught in school. Maybe the most important lessons are learned outside the classroom. I suppose I'm learning something now.

Who comes up with these rules, anyway? Can I rip out ears? Bite his nose? Stick a finger in his eyes? Pull his hair? Somehow, all these were understood as verboten. Anathema. Taboo. Cheating. But was it fair that I got punched without warning? And without breakfast? I'm starving. Famished. I'm running on orange juice fumes. And I didn't even get to prepare. Pros get at least three months notice. Nathan probably has an inflatable punching bag in his room. Maybe his dad was a professional fighter. Ex-Golden Gloves. A former wrestler. My dad's a boar, but that's all tusks. I didn't inherit sharp weapons.

None of us studied the gentlemanly art of hand-to-hand combat. Sure, we'd goof around, but that wasn't real fighting. We played with pretend swords more than fists. It's ironic that most kids don't prepare for schoolyard fights when they're the most likely age group to get into one. Some adults get into scuffles, too, but they go to jail. Kids get sent home with a note, hopefully sans black eye. I think I'm going to end up with both after this round.

If only this were a dream. Then I could wake up. It sort of feels like a dream. Unreal. Fantastical. Surreal. Actually, it's like a nightmare. But no monsters. And laser guns. I'm weaponless. If this is a dream, it's a real *sucky* one. I want to wake up. I want a do-over. Next time, I'll go in with guns blazing.

*   *   *

I wasn't stronger but I was quicker and nimbler. I twisted my body around and managed to push him off with my back. He tried to go for a guillotine but I escaped the chopping block. We were on our feet again. Pugilism standing up. *Bopp! Bopp!* I'm a punching bag. Maybe this wasn't a good idea.

By now, most of my nervousness had faded. I was just going through the motions. Survival on autopilot. My telescopic vision zoomed in on Goliath. The crowd was a blur. Punch. Swing. Jab. I was smacking his face, too. My hands didn't feel a thing. Aim for the eyes. Solar plexus. Nose. Body. *This ain't so hard, after all,* I thought. Then I heard, "Sam, don't stop punching!" It was Scott. Okay, just keep swinging. I'm a kid. I'm hungry but I also have boundless energy. This isn't a marathon. It's a sprint. I'm a windmill. I swung my fists like a sling. This must have been what it was like in the Old Testament. Or the savannas. Life was short and brutish. You're traipsing around one moment and then giant teeth interrupt your afternoon waltz. Who invited the lion? It's a war of *all against all.* Hey, I might be pretty good at this!

If only I had some formal training. Boxing. Karate. Kung-fu. Jiu-jitsu. Taekwondo. I wish I could jump in the air and deliver a three-hundred-sixty tornado kick. The mind is wishful, the body is clueless. For sure, I'm gonna start taking lessons. I think I was hitting Nathan but it didn't register. Luckily, I was fast and quick. My hands seemed to be going off more quickly than his. *Bopp. Bopp. Bopp.* I'm a machine gun.

*   *   *

When you're in *flow*, the world is said to disappear. It's just you and the ball, the racket, the basket, the field, and whatever you're doing *right now*. The self falls off and melts away. There is no thinking. No past. No future. Only now. Just this moment, *moment to moment*. Like an echo, you respond spontaneously. Naturally. In an instant. You're *everything* that's happening.

I'm the fist crashing into Nathan's face. I'm Nathan's grimace and left jab. I'm the violent dance, the gambol, on the schoolyard, more precarious than the rumba and the salsa. I'm all action. Pure verb. No subject or object. No *me*, no *not me*. No *my body*, no *not my body*. Just *flow*. They call it being *in the zone*.

Then, *kapow!* Right on the solar plexus. Or maybe the liver. The sound of collective surprise arose from the pubescent crowd. *"Waaahhhh!"* It was a beautiful liver shot. Is anyone recording this? Nathan bent over. He was hurt. Now what do I do? Give him time to recover? Take his head and declare victory? What's the rules? Does he get ten seconds? I hesitated. I stopped. I stared. I felt sorry. Why did I have to hit him so hard? If I had the killer instincts of a warthog, I would have impaled him. If this was 3000 BCE, his head would be on a stake. His face would decorate my wall. I'd take his nose as a souvenir.

When time almost seemed to return to normal, he recovered and glared at me with the eyes of a mad dog. He growled and jumped into the air and came raining down with punches and screams. I'm not sure what terrified me more. He tackled me and I was on my back again. *Thud.* Ouch! The pavement was hard. I hit my head on the ground. Nathan's a heavy boy. He obviously had a full breakfast. Probably bacon and eggs. I felt hungry again. Weak. Where did my energy go? I need a can of spinach. It seems we've been at this for an hour. How long is lunch?

* * *

Sometimes you just run out of energy. People talk about a second wind but it doesn't always come. Sometimes, the first wind is all you get. And then you collapse. I tried to budge him, but he wouldn't move. I tried to twist and turn over like I did last time. I didn't have the strength or quickness. I felt drained and exhausted. I didn't care about embarrassment or losing anymore. I wanted to go home and lie on my bed. I don't know if there was any victory to be had here.

Dad once said that boars never lose fights. They win or die on grassy fields. If it's not a lion, there are no excuses. Nathan was big, but just a boy. I'm supposed to have animal genes. Where's my animal strength? I must have left it at breakfast. I should blame Mom. Kids are supposed to have breakfast. She should know food better than anyone. According to the third law of thermodynamics, everything winds down. Maybe I'll just let Nathan tire himself out. I'm not sure I have much choice. This science thing better work.

He was just flailing at my arms now. My face was covered and it didn't hurt. I noticed a mouse under his eye. I gave him that. I imagine mine was worse. Probably rats hanging from my eyeballs. And raccoons camping out nearby. Why did he punch me again? I can't remember. How did this get started, anyway? Joey. I hardly know Joey. He was a smart alecky kid that was sometimes intentionally annoying. He needled classmates he probably shouldn't. This time, he poked a bear—Nathan. And I was paying for it because I wanted to be an upstanding guy. Oy vey! Bears have to eat, too. Not all prey are innocent. Sometimes they deserve to be eaten. I was looking forward to lunch. Today's menu was turkey stew and cornbread. My favorite. *Yum . . .*

9

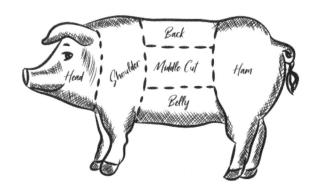

MOMMY PORK CHOPS

*"But what moral crime did these pigs commit? They were
only guilty of being delicious."*

Mom went to the market this morning and she
hasn't been back in four and a half hours. We
called her on the phone and no answer. Text, no
response. Twizzer, Instabram, Facebark, Giggool and
Snapshaft. No updates there either. We called Mr. Gonzales
at the butcher shop and she hasn't been in today. Strange. He
had seventy pounds of meat to unload. Mr. Gonzales was
concerned. Dad and I were starting to get worried. We know
she's a slow poke, but no one could be this slow. Something
was amiss. I need my milk and cereal.

Dad's anxious because it's a crazy world out there. There

are all kinds of lunatics that kidnap women, children, and even pigs. Mom's a full grown sow weighing more than most men, but she can be delicate and naive. She could be lured by bad people with false promises of sweet fruit and buttery potatoes. Suidae Valley is a safe town with friendly people, but there are bad apples everywhere.

We borrowed a neighbor's car and drove everywhere Mom could be. She was nowhere in sight. Her car was nowhere in sight. The supermarket on Fourth. Farmers market on Elm. Food4Pennies on Witchita. It's not a big town. There aren't a lot of places to go for grocery shopping.

"This isn't looking good, Sam," Dad confessed. "I'm really worried." He possessed an unusual calm when I would normally expect great perturbation.

"Maybe we should call the police?" I said.

"I'm afraid that's not going to be of any use, but we can try. They don't believe a missing pig is a 911 situation. They call it a job for animal services."

Was that possible? "That's inhumane!" I shouted. I was getting emotional.

"Son, we live in a wacky world. This town is called Suidae Valley but sometimes they just see us as one of the animals."

We continued searching into the night and we ran out of places to go except hills and mountains. We drove through dirt road, detours, and side streets. It was 2 a.m. At 3:06 a.m., we found our car. It was parked on a narrow road three and a half miles out of town. The keys were still in. Nothing seemed to be missing. But no Mom. No signs of struggle. Groceries in the rear seat. She hadn't finished shopping. No milk and cereal.

* * *

Next morning, Dad retrieved the car and we went to the police station to make an official report. But as expected, they referred us to animal services. 1-800-LOST-PIG. Dad had a conniption. He almost impaled the police officer with the dirty mouth. Eight men had to hold him back.

"That's my father! Let him go!" I yelled. I was feeling emotional again.

"It's okay, son. Breathe slow," the police chief said. I was hyperventilating. "Your father is a little animated. We'll let him go when he calms down. He thinks a pig is his wife."

"That's my mom! She's not an animal!" I remonstrated.

"It's a pig, son. Call animal services. 1-800-LOST-PIG." I kicked him in the shin and threatened to break his leg. He looked at me like I was on the spectrum. "Kid, are you Aspergers?"

When Dad stopped manhandling the officers, we were allowed to go free. We had to find Mom on our own.

Dad was a plumber, not a detective or bloodhound, but he could track down almost anything with his uber sense of smell. We returned to the spot where we found our car and he started to sniff around. I tried to see if I could smell anything, too, but my nose was only human. *"Achoooo!"* I inhaled sand and dirt. I was like a fish trying to sing.

"Just follow my lead, Sam. I'm gonna move fast!" Dad said.

He was on all fours. It was a throwback to old times. His snout was picking up all kinds of unusual scents, including Mom.

"Yup, Mom was definitely here. No doubt about it," he said grimly. She was musky with a hint of flowers and potatoes. There were also two other men. And apple pie. And bananas. They lured her with freshly baked apple pies and banana cake. But we had to be quick before we lost the trail.

He followed his nose through a narrow hilly corridor into a small valley divided by a stream. I had trouble keeping up. I was fast but no match for a feral warthog.

Dad guessed we were about four miles outside of Suidae Valley in the county of Bacon. As the name suggests, it was once a thriving community of pigs. But not residents, livestock. Chattel. They were once slaughtered here by the thousands. A Killing Fields of piggly proportions. But about thirty years ago the popularity of pork began to wane and farmers replaced pigs with chicken. Animals everywhere cheered, except poultry. Now, it was a chicken massacre. Poor birdies. Too bad they're so tasty. I think Mom makes chicken at least twice a week.

There were still a few traditionalists, and sometimes, you'll find a farmer raising pigs for pork chops and savory bacon. My friends tell me they're delicious. I reflexively retch but I try not to be obvious. Dad is afraid Mom might be salty bacon by now. In the old days, she would be a prize sow. Her left hind leg could feed students in several school districts for a week.

Dad followed where the musky scent led him and soon we spotted a small farm in the distance. We approached cautiously, and to our horror, it was a pig farm. Our hearts sank. About half a dozen farm pigs were playing in the dirty pen. Dad recognized Mom. She was up to her ears in mud. She looked happy. Maybe it was her version of the afterlife? Some people want to die and have seven wives. Mom wants to lark in the mud. She could be in shock. She didn't say a word of English except *oink!* Dad was in disbelief. I was confused and scared. Thoughts were crashing in my head and feelings were turning in my stomach like clothes in a laundry.

"Honey, honey . . . are you okay?!" Dad pleaded.

"Oink! Oink!"

"It's me! Your husband! Say something!"

"Oink! Oink!"

"Mom, it's me! Do you understand? We have to go home!" I begged.

"Oink! Oink!"

"Why did you forget milk and cereal?"

"Oink! Oink!"

Mom seemed to be speaking a form of pig Latin. Maybe the shock of the past couple days made her regress to an earlier form.

"Mom, are you speaking pig Latin?" I asked.

"Oink! Oink!"

"Ommay, reaay ouyay peakingsay igpay atinlay?" I was hoping my pig Latin could get through to her. "Ouya Orgotfay Ilkmay Nday Erealcay!"

"Oink! Oink!"

She didn't understand me. She was all *Oink! Oink!* and I couldn't decipher her code. None of it made any sense to me.

Then out of nowhere, "Hey there, stranger!" It was an old

farmer. "What can I help you with? You looking for something?" He sounded like someone who runs the place.

"That's my wife!" Dad shouted, pointing at Mom. "You have to release her pronto!" The farmer was flabbergasted. He'd heard of people marrying mail order brides and silicon robots, but never a pig.

"Your wife? Come on, mister. I don't know where you're from, but this is a pig. A prize sow. A British Lop. A fine pedigree from what I understand."

"I know that! She's also my wife—"

"And my mom!" I interjected. I was getting emotional again.

"Now, are you going to release her or do I have to impale you!" Dad threatened.

The farmer didn't seem to take well to threats, especially from a hairy, foreign looking man with tusks growing out of his face with a fidgety little kid at his side who looked like he might be on the spectrum. If I was close enough, I would have kicked him in the shin.

"Wait, see here! I don't like threats, stranger!" A shotgun emerged from the farmer's hands. "Boys!" The farmer's three sons appeared out of the background. They were armed with rifles.

Dad and I were in a bad spot, needless to say. We were out-gunned, four to zero. If only I had brought my BB gun. I might be able to shoot the old man right in the eye.

"The sow was purchased fair and legal," the old farmer insisted. "I have a bill of sale right here." He carefully reached into his pocket and pulled out an official looking piece of paper. It appeared to be an invoice for the sale of an oversized pig for three hundred dollars. "Two strangers came by yesterday and sold it to me."

Dad was outraged. He couldn't believe his wife was being bought and sold like livestock. Was it really the 21st century or the 20th? Are we back in medieval times? It was incredible how little we had progressed as a society and species.

"*Aaaaaargggghhhhh!*" Dad roared. "My wife is not livestock!" The four men cocked their triggers and aimed.

We were forced to back off. Dad could probably impale all four of them in five seconds, but I'd probably end up as dog meat. Dad was as tough as any wild warthog, but I was a soft little boy. Bullets go through me like cream filled donuts. It wasn't a chance Dad could take. I bleed easily.

Mom looked in our direction but nothing seemed to register. She was a farm pig playing in water and soft sand like an *arhat* bathing in liquid nirvana. The farmer said he was going to slaughter her for market tomorrow night. It was going to be a pork fest for the residents of Bacon. In her idyllic bliss, I doubt Mom was anticipating the frying pan.

* * *

We were determined to rescue Mom and returned to the farm that same night. I brought my BB gun and observed from a distance as Dad approached. But to our shocking surprise, the pig pen was being guarded by a dozen gunmen. It was useless. Dad could take care of a handful of men but a dozen was too many. Besides, Mom could get caught in the crossfire. We would have to figure out another way. But what?

We went to town for food and supplies. Mom was kidnapped and held like a Taliban hostage but she was unharmed for now. No chopping off heads tonight. Some had heard rumors about the kidnapping but wavered. Morally, it was wrong, they conceded. Mom was a member of the community, but technically, she was a pig. The civil rights of swine are limited. There was nothing against the law barring the sale of pigs and the manufacture of pork chops and bacon. No one knew quite what they could do to help except offer their condolences. The farmers in Bacon County were also tough cowboys. Stealing chattel was a felony. And local ordinances gave farmers the right to shoot trespassers on the spot.

Dad plotted to go it alone and rescue Mom Rambo style. However, the town counsel implored him to attend an ad hoc meeting tomorrow morning. The mayor, counsel members, concerned citizens, and the best lawyers in town would also be present.

*   *   *

"Legally, there aren't a lot of options," a lawyer with a long goatee said. "Livestock don't have rights."

The meeting was underway to discuss Mom's kidnapping situation. A lot of people from town showed up, including a few of my teachers from school.

"My wife is not livestock!" Dad yelled. "I will not have you referring to my wife as a farm animal!"

"Yes, of course. Mr. Waters, please choose your words more carefully," councilman Buranosky admonished.

"Sorry, Mr. Swine," the lawyer said regretfully.

The mayor asked his staff if anyone has been able to contact their peers in Bacon. A college intern stood up and said he had, but no luck. The deputy mayor of Bacon refused to turn over Mrs. Swine. He didn't care that she was married to Mr. Swine and had a little boy. He said the town needed the pork chop revenues and Bacon farmers had legal rights to property just like chicken and cow farmers.

"The logical thing would be to prove that Mrs. Swine is not chattel," Mr. McCoy, my math teacher, said. "That would bring the law to our side." *But how?* everyone wondered.

"There might be a legal precedent—if she can talk," another lawyer added. She was a twenty-something attorney who specialized in immigration law and domestic abuse. She was pretty but didn't seem to have a chin in side profile.

"But she's in shock and can't talk!" Dad hollered. "She just mutters gibberish!"

"Maybe we could arouse her into speaking again?" suggested Mr. Johnson, my history teacher. "With her favorite food. Or with a reminder of her previous life. History is replete with stories of memories coming back."

"What's all this talk about rescuing a pig?" interrupted Ms. Fearstein, my English teacher. "Off with her head! Let her roast! I love pork chops!"

A collective gasp arose. The mayor asked her to leave. She

was a very bad woman. But she didn't leave without protestation. "This is discrimination! Intolerance! Fascism! Thought police! 1984 all over again!" When I returned to class, she would tell us that she is a champion of free speech, the First Amendment, and the open exchange of ideas. She encouraged us all to speak our minds and exercise our rights. Except when she disagreed.

"Look, we're doing a lot of jabbering while my wife is being held hostage by ISIS," Dad exclaimed. "I say we go in there like Dirty Harry and take the radical farmers down like Wolverine. Who's with me?"

"I'm with you, Mr. Swine," a voice said. "Me too! You can count on me!" said another man. The chorus grew to a clamor. Dad had lots of support from ordinary citizens.

"Wait! Wait! Innocent people could get hurt if we do that!" the mayor begged. "Those farmers aren't pushovers. They have shotguns. Have you seen what a shotgun can do to a man?"

"Turn him into Swiss cheese, including possibly Mrs. Swine," Ms. Jones, my health teacher, answered. "It seems to me that if we can find the kidnappers and demonstrate that Mrs. Swine was absconded unlawfully, then the farmer's bill of sale would be null and void. If only we had a clue about the two men. Is there any information about them?"

Everyone shook their heads—except Mr. Gonzalez, the butcher, who suddenly raced into the meeting, huffing and puffing.

"I think I know who did it!" Mr. Gonzales announced, slumped over and catching his breath. "My six cousins in Bacon just told me about two suspicious men bragging about stealing a pig at a bar last night. They must be the evil hombres!"

"Who? Where? Tell me, Jose!" Dad shouted. "I'll massacre them!"

"Now, please calm down," councilman Buranosky implored. "We'll form a posse to find them."

"I don't know if there's enough time," the lawyer with the goatee said. "Barbecue is tonight."

"We'll have to split up," suggested Mr. Johnson. "Some of us will have to go to the farm and try to reason with the men and buy some time while Jose takes a posse to apprehend the kidnappers."

Dad agreed to the plan but also warned that if worst comes to worst, he'd have to take matters into his own hoofs. People will get hurt. There's no way he was going to let his wife become pork chops. "These horns weren't made for just digging root vegetables," he said.

* * *

A posse of tough guys was assembled, and with Mr. Gonzales taking the lead, they headed out for Bacon to meet up with his six cousins in search of the two men. Hopefully, they would find the bandits, force a confession, and return to the farm in time to forestall a preamble to a funeral.

Dad and the rest of the concerned citizens prepared to confront the armed farmers. We didn't know if Mr. Gonzales would succeed. But we had to do our best to buy time, and if things came to a head, do what we could to save Mom. Everyone understood that this was a potentially dangerous mission. There could be collateral damage. I hid a sling shot in my pocket just in case things turned messy.

When we came to the farm, our hearts collectively dropped. The slaughter had begun. Blood was everywhere. We drove quickly and rushed to the scene. Four pigs had been killed. Another was on the chopping block. Where was Mom? I was frantic. Dad was furious. The rest of the group with us were glum. It seems we might have wasted too much time discussing the situation and too little doing something about it.

Then Mom's head popped up from the mud. She was playing peek-a-boo.

"Oink! Oink!" she said.

"Gaddarnit, honey! We thought you were dead!" Dad cried.

The area was crawling with armed gunmen. The next poor animal on the chopping block was squealing like a pig on its way to execution. The farmers had a very simple setup. Place the pig's head over the chopping block, and then, *whack!* With a giant cleaver that looked more like a sword, kill it in one clean stroke. It was like Saudi Arabia on the weekends. But what moral crime did these pigs commit? They stole nothing. They were only guilty of being delicious.

"Stand back, folks!" a gunman commanded. "Another pig is going to be separated from its head!"

My stomach was turning and doing flips. We all watched with consternation and dreaded anticipation. These pigs were livestock. But what were we going to do when it's Mom's turn?

WHACK!

It was a clean slice. The pig's head rolled down the platform into a barrel. In twenty-four hours it would become SPAM and enjoyed by thousands of Hawaiians. The body was then divided into its constituent parts. The expert farmers worked swiftly. The backside would be cut into ham. The middle would become bacon for someone's breakfast. The spareribs would be barbecue on Labor Day. The shoulders would be roast for dinner. And the feet could be used in soups and stews. It was like the time we sliced open a frog at school and cut it into pieces. Except we didn't eat it, and a pig is a hundred times bigger. And as far as I know, there are no frogs in our family.

It was now Mom's turn and six gunmen approached the pen. Dad blocked their path.

"Step away, mister!" the farmer commanded.

"Farmer boy, this is my wife. And if you want her, it'll be over my dead body," Dad warned. His sharp tusks hovered millimeters from the farmer's head. It could become jack o' lantern in half a second.

"Please, everyone!" the mayor yelled in appeal to the farmers. "I'm the mayor of Suidae Valley. We're neighbors. We don't want anyone to get hurt. We just ask for a short delay."

Then the old farmer came forward and exhorted us not to interfere. "We have buyers coming in a few hours. We have to get this sow ready for market. Sorry. No can delay."

"There's a dozen of us," said Mr. Johnson. "We're average folks. Your neighbors. We're asking you to give us a little time. I don't think you want to kill us all, do you?"

"No, I sure don't. But I'm sure as heck not going let anyone tell me what I can and can't do on my farm. Let me also remind you that you're on private property. Now, step back!"

"Please, give us a little time," begged Ms. Jones and a number of other co-ed members. The old farmer wasn't a pushover but even men like him can't ignore a pretty, misty eyed woman. "We might be able to prove that this pig doesn't belong here. The sale was unlawful. She was kidnapped."

"I think it's all foolish nonsense. It's against my better judgment, but I'll give you folks an hour," granted the farmer.

A sigh of relief arose from our side. But would an hour be enough? Would Mr. Gonzalez be able to find the robbers in time?

The adults discussed among themselves various contingency scenarios but nothing was satisfactory. Risks abounded at every turn. We couldn't fight them. That would be against the law, in fact. And the armed gunmen stood between us and Mom. We were unable to get close to her. The minutes ticked. And then time ran out. The hour was up.

"Alright, folks, stand back and make room," shouted the old farmer. "The hour's elapsed and we are now going to proceed as planned. Please don't try to get in the way or someone is likely to get hurt!"

"We're really sorry about this, Mr. Swine," said the mayor in the way of condolences, placing his hands on Dad's hairy shoulder. "I don't think there's anything more we can do."

"I appreciate the effort," Dad said. "I'm grateful so many

of you folks came out here in support. Please take my son with you. Now, I'll have to do what I have to."

The gunmen waved the rest of us back but Dad remained in front. No one was sure exactly what he was planning. Maybe he was thinking of a scene from Rambo. Or Dirty Harry. Or Conan the Barbarian. But Dad had horns, not guns. They had rifles. Guns beat horns almost every time.

One of the farmers led Mom up to the platform to be sliced and diced luring her with ears of corn. Poor Mom. Her mouth was full. She was smiling. But she didn't have a clue what was about to happen to her. She just oinked and trotted up the steps.

But like Dad, I hadn't given up either. I collected a handful of big, solid stones from the ground and pulled the slingshot from my pocket. When the time was right, I slipped and crouched in between legs.

Dad vacillated between threats of total destruction and friendly relations, including discounted plumbing repairs, if the farmers let Mom go. But the old man was neither intimidated nor interested in discounted plumbing. He was a Vietnam soldier back in the day and he was familiar with blood and gore. No oversized warthog was going to scare him even though Dad could snap his neck before he could say Saigon.

As the farmers on the stage struggled to get Mom in place with her mouthful of corn, Dad's voice escalated louder and louder. Soon, war of words became a tussle. Dad grabbed the old man's rifle, and the two began to push and pull. The other farmers tried to help and pry Dad away. But no use. Dad was a beast. Too strong.

In modern warfare, it's often not diplomacy that makes the rules but the guy with the biggest guns. With that view, guerrilla warfare can be useful. Could I be of service? I thought I might tip the tête-à-tête a little in Dad's favor by knocking the farmer's rifle off his hands with my slingshot.

I loaded my rock, pulled, aimed, steadied my hands, and then released. It was a beautiful shot! Except, it missed the farmer's rifle by an inch, zoomed past him, and hit of all people, my own mother! I got her right on the schnozzle. Mom was stunned and went ballistic. She jumped and squealed and hopped around the platform like a loon in a loony bin.

The farmer's were beside themselves. She was a wild beast. An angry bull. They couldn't get her to calm down. She was too big and too strong. She was bouncing and jerking like a pig twerking on a hot frying pan.

In the middle of the chaos, the mayor and others received a text message from Mr. Gonzales that he was on his way! They had found the robbers and forced a confession. We would have the proof we needed to show that it was an unlawful sale.

Dad pushed aside the old man and ran to the platform to calm Mom down. Now there were two overgrown pigs jumping on top of the platform and the weight was just too much. The structure began to give way. Suddenly, everything collapsed and both Mom and Dad came crashing down. *KABOOM!* A mushroom cloud of dust arose as if an atomic bomb was dropped. It was like Hiroshima all over again.

Dad landed on his butt. He was okay. But Mom landed on her head and she was concussed into a daze. When she came to, however, she looked around in total confusion.

"What in the world is going on here?!" she yelled. The oinking had stopped. She was speaking normal again.

The farmers gasped. A talking pig! They had never seen a talking pig. This could only mean that she wasn't livestock. Not a farm animal at all, but almost human.

"Honey, you're back!" Dad screamed. "You were almost pork chops for a second!"

"Pork chops? Who gave anyone permission to turn me into pork chops?"

"You were kidnapped and you lost your memory. You couldn't speak a word except *oink!*"

In the distance, a caravan was approaching at high speed. It was Mr. Gonzales and his posse! And two men were in the backseat of the truck in handcuffs.

"Them!" Mom exclaimed. "They're the men that promised me rack of lamb at seventy percent discount and hit me over the head! Why those two!"

"Do you recognize these men, Mrs. Swine!" asked Jose, leaping from the speeding truck.

"Yes, I certainly do. You two men are BAD. Real BAD!"

"I think we made a terrible mistake, Mrs. Swine," said the old farmer. "We thought you were a prize hog."

"I am a prize pig. A British Lop. I'm sure you paid a handsome fortune for me, right? How much did you buy me for?"

"Three hundred," replied the farmer.

"Is that all!" Mom was irate. "The nerve! I've never been so insulted!" She couldn't believe she was sold at a discount like a common pleb.

"My apologies, mam. I didn't mean to besmirch your dignity," said the farmer. "I should have paid a lot more."

"Next time, you need to know the fair value of a prize hog when you see one!" admonished an angry Mom. "Pigs like me are rare! Do you know how delicious I am?"

"I wish I knew, mam . . . I really do . . ." the farmer said with undisguised regret.

* * *

Mom came home and took a long deserved rest. She was so well fed on the farm, actually, she gained a bit of weight. Nonetheless, Dad said she should lose it naturally with good homemade food. No crash starvation diets. Mom strongly agreed.

The police arrested the two men who kidnapped Mom. The detective on the case assured us that they had plenty of evidence, including a confession. And they would be prosecuted to the fullest extent of the law. After all, we can't have pig thieves in a town called Suidae Valley.

I was glad to see Mom back home, safe and sound. The last couple days were very emotional. I lost sleep. My appetite. And fell behind on my assignments. I would have some catching up to do. My teachers said they'd give me time to make up for lost work. But Ms. Fearstein said it wouldn't be fair to make exceptions just for me. After all, it's not her fault I'm autistic.

I never confessed that it was me that hit Mom on the

schnozzle and made her go nutso. If I do, I'm afraid it might bring back horrible memories. Even worse, invite an earful of unnecessary yelling, shouting, and reprimands. There are signs Mom could be suffering from PTSD. She's pensively quiet. And resting in her room, lounging in her mud bath, she sometimes wistfully looks away into the distance, as if yearning and pining, for paradise lost.

10

FAIR WEATHER FRIEND

*"In the wild, ostracized animals die. Did I want
to sentence the monkey to death?"*

I saw Ricky sitting alone in the cafeteria having his peanut butter and jelly sandwich. He spotted me and unctuously waved hello. I wasn't sure I should return the salutation. It wasn't my first time at the rodeo with Ricky Geraldo. We used to be pretty good friends in grammar school.

"Sam! Over here! It's me, Ricky!" As if I wouldn't know who he is.

Ricky is what you might call a "fair weather friend." Not a lot of sticky loyal marrow in his bones. When the pot boils, he tends to jump out. Maybe he has very sensitive marrows? It's not the worst thing in the world, perhaps. People's natural instincts are to survive and climb, they say. But it's not the contract friends usually sign up for. He's not malicious, just self-interested and instinctively self-serving, I think. He's a pretty good friend when things are swell, but he turns tail as soon as the grass looks greener on the other side or things turn brown in his. Or maybe I'm totally wrong about him. It's not easy interpreting these things.

"Hola, Ricky. What's up?"

"Not much. I quit the Gamers Club. Dorks! My lunch periods are finally free. What a relief! Where are you going?"

It seemed Ricky was on the outs with his erstwhile school buddies. The story is that he tried to rig the Gamers Club elections for president by stuffing the ballot box. They found thirty tickets. There are just fifteen members in the club. Sixteen votes went to Mr. Geraldo. No one could prove it, but he was the only possible suspect. Ricky screamed foul and accused his opponent of planting evidence. It was an awkward situation among geeks. The club said they had no choice but to evict him given his stubborn recalcitrance and serial mendacity. Knowing Ricky since the second grade, I can't say I'm surprised.

"Just gonna meet Danny and Scott over on the other side," I said.

"We haven't seen each other in such a long time! We should hang out," Ricky said, probing for an invitation.

The Gamers Club played video games during lunchtime and after school. They also competed against rival schools in regional eSport leagues every quarter. There was no official sponsorship by the school besides the use of the computer room. It was just for fun. Something for nerds to do during lunch while foraging on baloney sandwiches and sipping apple juice. But in one afternoon, Ricky lost his lunch buddies and temporal circle of friends. He was like a baboon ousted from his troop. He needed new jungle mates.

"We're gonna have lunch and do some homework—"

"Me, too!" Ricky interjected. He put his sandwich in his brown bag, gathered his belongings, and accosted me. It all happened so fast.

"Let's go!" he said, smiling. Ricky must have grown at least a head taller over summer. How much baloney do you have to eat to acquire that?

"I'm really sorry about getting back to you late with the text messages," he apologized as we walked. He shuffled his feet and shortened his gait to match my pace. "I was going through a phase." The last text message I sent him was almost two years ago.

In the fourth grade, Ricky and I went to a friend's birthday party at Zhuck F. Cheese's. Within an hour, he was missing. We found him at Dave & Rooster's next door at another party. Ricky didn't seem to think there was anything wrong going to another kid's party. He said he was only next door. He would be back in time for cake and free prizes.

"Hey, guys!" Ricky offered, his raised open hand revealing no weapons or gifts. Danny and Scott looked surprised. They hadn't talked to Ricky in years. In adult calendar, decades.

"What's up, Ricky?" Danny returned in greeting. Scott just nodded his head. He was feeling discombobulated by the foreign presence.

We all used to be friends in grammar school. But during a Math Bowl competition in the fifth grade, Ricky deserted our group to join a different one with nerdier kids leaving us a member short. We thought it was treason and betrayal. Ricky said he just wanted to be part of a winning team. We were bad at math. Nothing personal. We didn't do well that year.

Now he wanted reentry. What do you do when a former friend, now friendless, imposes himself? In the wild, ostracized animals die. Social animals need a community of support to survive. Did I want to sentence the monkey to death?

* * *

We hadn't quite digested the circumstances of the day before. I wasn't sure what to make of Ricky and the guys didn't seem keen on him sticking around. To our dread, Ricky was spotted at our lunch table. He was waiting for us. We had to make a decision.

"Let's sit somewhere else," said Danny.

"But why should we hide? We did nothing wrong," said Scott.

He had a point. The innocent shouldn't have to hide. But in the real world, it's often the brazen that impose themselves.

"You really want to do that? Ricky is probably waiting for us," I said.

"Yeah, I know, that's why we should sit somewhere else!" Danny said.

They say everyone deserves a second chance. Steve Pobs got a second chance and created the ePhone. Maybe Ricky will be different this time around. Maybe he's acquired a new vista on life, at least a head-size higher?

Danny cut a path toward a table with a gap. It was unfamiliar territory with neighbors we didn't know. We were taking up space long staked out by other kids. But what could we do? We were homeless and forced ourselves in between girls who aspired to look like Hello Kitty and members of the army ROTC.

"Sorry, guys, someone took our seats," I confessed.

"That's Mary's seat!" a chunky girl with pointy feline ears said.

"Is she really wide? I don't take up a lot of space," Danny entreated, trying to negotiate temporary asylum.

"No! She's small as me. But that's her seat."

The ROTC was more accommodating. They squeezed in together like good troops to make room for us. Maybe it was the unstated creed of wannabe soldiers to look kindly on refugees. Or maybe they welcomed a friendly buffer zone between humans and cats.

"Aren't you the fastest runner in school?" one of the ROTC kids asked. He was wearing green fatigues and decked out in aspirational medals.

"Yeah, I am. Probably," I answered.

"We could use guys like you. You should join the ROTC."

While I was having a tête-à-tête with the military brass, Scott picked up a conversation with a nicer feline. It turned out she was a patient of his father.

"I just saw your dad yesterday!" the fury creature said before taking another bite of rice from her *bento* box. "He said I have perfect teeth. Not a single cavity."

"Really? Let me see! Open your mouth!" joked Scott.

"Gross!" the others shrieked. Cats are predatory animals but maybe this litter found a friendly tom.

"Have you ever tried *wasabi?*" a girl with whiskers asked.

Scott shook his head and a California roll was promptly offered pinched between pairs of chopsticks dripping with green sauce. When he took it in his mouth a caterwaul of laughter exploded. Scott was in big trouble!

One good thing about foreign territory is that you can make new friends. Or as Danny found out, new enemies. The girl with pointy ears was still giving him malevolent sideway glances. I was trying to avoid the draft.

* * *

We had to make a decision about Ricky. We couldn't avoid the kid forever. We had to man up and tell the monkey *yes* or *no*. He was looking glum and depressed. I think he knew we were avoiding him. He stopped inviting himself to our lunch area and sat alone grazing on a tuna sandwich at an abandoned table long forsaken by potheads.

"What's up, Ricky?" I said, approaching him diagonally.

"Hey! I haven't seen you in a while. Where have you guys been?" His frown suddenly turned upside down.

"We've been around. Busy with basketball," I explained, which wasn't a lie. The playoffs were coming up, and our team, the Raptors, practiced after school everyday. It was me,

Danny, Scott, a kid named Joe, who was a great three point shooter despite his asthma, and Pete, our point man and phenom on the piano. He had a recital coming up but we didn't expect it to conflict with our games.

"It must be fun!" Ricky said. I wasn't sure whether he was excited by basketball or not being alone anymore.

"It's fun and a lot of practice and pressure. It's an elimination playoff, which means you have to win every game to make it to the finals. With your length and height, I bet you could be a pretty good basketball player!" I was looking for a way to compliment him and brighten his day.

"Ya think? Thanks! You're a nice friend."

Unexpectedly, pangs of guilt washed through my body like an icy wave. I felt like an impostor. When he called me a *nice friend* the words tugged at my heart. I felt bad because I really wasn't a nice friend. I had wished he would go away. But at that moment I wanted to give him another chance.

"Why are you sitting here all by yourself? Come on! Let's go have lunch at our table." Ricky's eyes lit up.

"Really? Yah!" He was giddy.

The guys weren't too happy with my solo decision but they eventually came around. They agreed that we couldn't keep ignoring Ricky, a former friend, now all alone like a mangy dog without a pack. He might betray us again but he could use some company in the meantime. We could at least give him that for old times' sake. Every hound deserves a bone.

∗   ∗   ∗

Ricky soon became a regular member of the gang. We hung out together for lunch and met up regularly after school for b-ball practice and study grinds at the library. He came to our practice games, too, and started to learn how to play. Ricky was still getting used to his length but with some help from the rest of the team, he was becoming a threat at center. He was an official unofficial member of the team.

"Good practice, guys!" Danny said. "You too, Ricky."

"Thanks, Danny!" Ricky said. "I didn't know basketball could be so much fun."

For a gangly kid, Ricky was picking up the game quickly. To be sure, he had a big height advantage. He was easily one of the tallest kids in school.

Unexpectedly, Pete got a text message from his mother. It was bad news. The venue for the recital had been moved to San Francisco. Pete would have to miss a few days of school. We'd have to find a replacement for the first two games.

"What's wrong, Pete?" Scott asked.

"Oh, boy. Bad news. My recital is going to be in San Francisco! Mom says I'm gonna have to miss two or three days of school. Maybe more. She's not sure."

"What?!" exclaimed Joe. "But we need you for the game!"

"Yeah, I know. I don't know what I'm going to do. Sorry guys." We all stood dejected and dumbstruck.

"Maybe Ricky can fill in?" I suggested. The guys weren't so sure but there didn't seem to be much of a choice. "What about it, Rick?"

Ricky was apprehensive but agreed. He said he'd do his best and practice hard the next couple days.

"If you guys want me. I'll do whatever I can to help out the team!" he promised. He was equally nervous and excited.

*   *   *

Our first game was a nail biter but we managed to eke out a win. Scott made three layups. Joe delivered with 5 three pointers despite asthma attacks in the middle of the game. Danny pulled seven rebounds. Ricky gave us two blocked shots and two layups. And five turnovers. But I made the lucky winning basket at the buzzer. After the game, Dad took us out for pizza.

"Great game, boys! When I was your age, football was my thing. *Wahhooo!* Hey, you. Kid in the middle. You look kinda familiar."

"It's me, Ricky," he said. "I used to wear glasses. I have contacts now."

"Oh, yeah . . . I haven't seen you in a while. Where have you been?"

"I've been around. I was sort of in the gaming club."

"Oh, you're one of those video game nerds!"

"He used to be, Dad," I chimed. "He's playing b-ball with us now."

"That's good. Those kids are dorks."

"I play center, Mr. Swine," Ricky said.

"*Ooooohhh!* Important position! I used to be linebacker."

"He's getting really good, Mr. Swine," said Joe. "No one can stop him at center!"

"Thanks, Joe. I couldn't have done it without you guys, of course."

"He scored four points, Mr. Swine. Maybe he'll go pro someday!" said Danny.

"Well, he might if he keeps growing like bamboo. Hahahaha!" Dad howled.

"The next game is going to be tough," said Scott. "We're all going to have to play better . . ."

It seemed Ricky wasn't an ostracized baboon anymore. He was an official member of the Raptors and back in the fold with Danny, Scott, and I. We filled our ravenous bellies at Pizza Palace, and Dad dropped the guys off at home. It was a good day to be a kid.

* * *

Ricky continued to improve his game. We tried to focus him on easy layups, rebounds, and block shots. We didn't want him to run around and tire himself out. He didn't have too much stamina. Ten minutes in and he was already exhausted. His strength was predominantly in the fingers. We wanted him to stand under the basket and wait for the pass. It was a simple strategy.

Our next game was against a team who called themselves the Lakers but they didn't have a tall Kareem. We sort of did sans sky hook, talent, and skills. We expected a tough game but it turned out easier than we thought. We passed the ball to Ricky and he went for the quick layup. Easy as Pong. They didn't have an answer for it. We trounced the Lakers 16 to 24.

"That was fantastic, Ricky!" I congratulated.

"Thanks. I think I might be getting a knack for the game!"

They say friendships are hard to measure when everything is going well. It's hard times, like receding hair lines, that reveal the skin underneath. Things may be good now, but like hair, there will be bad days. Mom says we all have bad hair days. She has a lot of bad hair days.

"You sure are, big man!" said Danny. "Maybe we have a chance to make it to the finals after all!"

Pete's trip to San Francisco was stretching to a week. He was busy playing Bach, Chopin, and Haydn before music aficionados that could offer him a scholarship to Juilliard in NYC. Frankly, Pete wasn't that interested but his tiger mom wanted nothing more.

* * *

Our next match was really going to be a tough one. We hoped we didn't draw them until later in the series. They had a tall, experienced center that would neutralize any height advantage offered by Ricky. The rest of us didn't have much of a chance with the remaining lineup as well. They were one of a couple teams expected to make it to the finals. The odds were heavily against us. This would probably be our last game.

Curiously, Ricky missed the following practice game. We tried to get a hold of him but no answer. We didn't think much of it until the next day when he didn't show up for lunch either. Actually, he was at lunch but with a different crowd.

The Knicks, as they called themselves, won the championship last year but their man was injured. They needed a new center. It seems they were on the scout for a new player and Ricky assumed he was a free agent. Friendships don't come with binding contracts but they never do.

"Hey, what's going on here?" I said. "Why weren't you at practice?"

"Hi . . . Sam," said Ricky, ever so slightly embarrassed. "These are my friends. This is Joel. This is James. And this is Michael."

"Your *friends?*"

"Yeah, they want me to play on their team."

"But you have a team. You know Pete won't be back for the next game."

"Yeah, I know. I'm really sorry about that. But he'll be back for the game after that, right?"

"Maybe, but if we lose a game in the tournament, we're out. You know that."

"Just find a temporary replacement. Besides, you said yourself that you didn't expect to win."

"How?! It's not like borrowing a book from the library!" I was rapidly losing my temper. "And that's not the point. We ought to just give it our best shot *as a team.*"

"Hey, man. Don't be sore!" interrupted James. "He just wants to play for the winning team. Playing for us means a trophy this year and fast-track to varsity basketball in a couple years."

"Alright, that's in two years. This year, he should be playing for us. What do you say, Ricky? Come on . . ."

"I'm really sorry, Sam. These guys need me. You're going to lose anyway with or without me. And I think I might have a future in basketball with these guys. You know, it's nothing personal."

"Holy mother of Snoopy!" I yelled. I couldn't believe Ricky did it to us again.

Actually, I could believe it intellectually but refused to believe it emotionally. I had started to reinvest in our friendship. And my investment had gone bust. I marched off.

I told the guys and they were angry, but not surprised. We thought we'd make Ricky into Steve Pobs but we forgot that Steve Pobs was a ruthless businessman. A lot of bodies were killed and buried to make those shiny new ePhones.

We didn't know how we were going to proceed with one man short. The only hope was for Pete to get back early. That wasn't likely.

*   *   *

We convinced Johnny to step in but he was too portly to contribute much. When he dribbled the ball, his tummy kept getting in the way. It was like out of control adipose jello. He turned over the ball seven times and made four air balls. We begged him to pass the ball, but he refused to listen. Maybe the excitement went to his head? His body wasn't used to exercise and too little oxygen in the brain made him stupid. We got eliminated in a blowout. Raptors 12. Celtics 44.

The Knicks made it to the finals but lost the match to the Celtics. It was pretty close but they blamed it on "clumsy Ricky." Under suffocating pressure and surrounded by more experienced players, he mentally broke and repeatedly committed errors. He was kicked off the team. They revoked his fast-track to varsity.

Ricky tried to get back with us with his dog tail between his legs, but the guys barked him away. They'd run out of patience for treachery. A second amnesty would not be granted. They could bear the wound of losing but not multiple acts of perfidy. We were supposed to be a team but Ricky tried to leave for greener pastures when it suited him. And now he wanted back. "We don't need backstabbing friends like you!" Danny shouted.

When he walked away, I felt sorry for the guy. Why did he do that? Again? It was hard to understand. Maybe some people just can't help themselves. It's like chronic liars, eaters and cheaters. They know it's wrong, but they do it anyway. They can't put down the cake, tell the truth, and play their cards straight. Something in them mysteriously pulls, pushes, and twists. They can't control themselves. It's like a self-driving Tislu that suddenly veers to the left and crashes into the freeway barrier. You just scratch your head and wonder how Emon Lusk went so wrong.

For the next couple weeks, I saw Ricky sitting alone at lunch. Then he migrated to the bleachers outside. And then he disappeared. I didn't know where he went. I looked around but couldn't find him in the cafeteria, the field, or bleachers. Later I learned that he somehow managed to wiggle his way back into the Gamers Club. They decided to give him a second chance. The scandal would be water under the bridge. Besides, Ricky was a good player, and they weren't doing so well in the regional competitions without him. Suidae Valley's reputation was tanking like Tislu stocks.

I saw him a couple times and said hello. He politely said hello back but didn't seem very interested in stopping and chatting. He had mentally and emotionally moved on. We had become strangers again. We were like a divorced couple walking past each other in the halls pretending our marriage was only a dream. It's our second divorce.

Hopefully things work out better for Ricky this time around. Underneath it all, he is a nice kid. Too bad he's just a *fair weather friend*. Not a lot of loyal marrow in his bones.

11

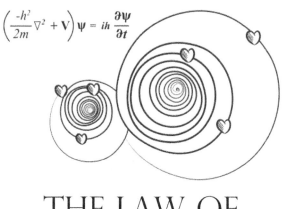

$$\left(\frac{-h^2}{2m}\nabla^2 + \mathbf{V}\right)\psi = ih\,\frac{\partial\psi}{\partial t}$$

THE LAW OF ATTRACTION

"You put an idea into the air and it cascades throughout time and space."

My mom thinks she found the answer to everything. It lies in a little secret called the *Law of Attraction*. The way it works, she explains, is that you think of something and then it happens. Voila! Seriously. But it can't just be a passing or momentary thought, but a firm belief. You have to put your whole mind and body into it. I tried it this morning but I still had to go to school. I really put my feeling into it. I yelled and screamed. There was lots of emotional drama. I used my entire body, too. I refused to get out of bed. But Mom dragged me out from under the covers and told me that her Law of Attraction was stronger than mine.

I went to school and told my math teacher, Mr. McCoy, about the Law of Attraction. He told me it was all *phooey*.

"Sam, the world is ruled by laws, but not laws of attraction, mathematical laws. One plus one is always equal to two, no matter what you think it is."

"Then why do people believe in the Law of Attraction?"

"Because they're *pinheads!*"

"But my mom says it's true."

"Women! *No offense girls.* It's just cockamamie nonsense to avoid working. They just want to avoid the law of labor. They want pie in the sky. A free lunch."

"Mr. McCoy, I don't believe in the Law of Attraction," Victoria volunteered. "I believe in being smart."

"That's good, Victoria. There's nothing men like more than smart women," Mr. McCoy said wryly.

"Mom said that if you think of something, you can change the fabric of the universe," I continued, attempting to wrest back the conversation. "You put an idea into the air and it cascades throughout time and space. It begins to reproduce and has babies."

"Well, Sam. Your mom is full of baloney. If you think a thought, it goes no farther than the diameter of your head. Ideas don't float around and multiply. That happens only in cartoons."

I mentioned the Law of Attraction to my English teacher, Ms. Fearstein, and she was adamant this was true. "Sam, I never liked you. But the Law of Attraction is spot on!"

What?!

"Ms. Fearstein, why don't you like me?"

"Well, Sam. It's the Law of Attraction. I'm not attracted to you. It's the law."

"How?! Why is that the law?"

"Because like attracts like. You and I are different. So we repel like two opposing magnets."

"Is there a way to turn the magnets around so they attract?"

"No. That would be illegal!"

I couldn't understand it. It made no sense. Ms. Fearstein was so *mean*.

"I'm attracted to you," Laura whispered.

"Ummm . . . thanks," I said awkwardly. I didn't expect that.

∗ ∗ ∗

Mom set up a *vision board* in her room. A vision board was something she hung on the wall with all the things she wanted to attract pinned to it. *Pinhead?* She had photos of big, juicy watermelon, monster sized sweet potatoes, a queen size mud bath, an immaculate kitchen, a perfectly manicured garden, a bikini ready body, a handsome husband, a big new house, brand new minivan, a diamond ring, a pearl necklace, Guffi bags, words like "happiness," "peace," "serenity," "patience," "gratefulness," and many other weird things.

"What in the world is that!" Dad exclaimed.

"It's my vision board."

"Vision what?! Who is *THAT* guy?"

"That's you. New and improved. Quieter."

"New house, kitchen, diamonds . . . is there anything you don't want?"

"Well, I have big dreams," Mom said. "Don't try to rain on my *positivity!*"

"If you're so positive, how can I get it wet? Grab an umbrella. Put on a raincoat. If you're so happy, why do you need all that stuff? Look at me. I'm perfectly content just as I am. *Wahhhoooo!*" Dad ran off with his hands raised in the air and making a lot of noise. He was apparently the champion of something.

Maybe Dad had a point. He said he was happy just as he was and didn't need a thing. But could it be that's also why he never changed? No evolution. He was stuck where he was. Want and desire, despite its drawbacks, have a way of moving the needle. Like love, fear, and anger, *emotions goad.*

Mom's big vision board reminded her of everything she wanted, but every time she looked at it, it served as an implicit cue of her lack and unfulfilled dreams. It made her a little sad. What's going on? Was there a way to be happy, content, and get new stuff too? Can we be happy now but want more happiness at the same time? It seemed like an intractable paradox.

Mom didn't have all the answers. She was only on chapter five of her book. She searched on the internet, forums, and user groups. *CAN YOU BE HAPPY NOW BUT STILL WANT MORE STUFF?* Punters and self-acclaimed experts seemed to disagree.

If there's an answer, it was anything but straightforward.

Somehow, you had to feel you already had the stuff, even though you didn't have the stuff. You had to make believe you were everything you wanted to be. Right now. You had to feel you are what you aren't and thereby attract what you already had but really didn't. *What?*

* * *

Mom became a new woman. She walked around in a bathing suit, though there was no pool. And no bikini body. She borrowed my basketball and made believe it was a giant sweet potato. She slobbered her slime all over it. She went into the kitchen to admire how clean and pristine it was, except it was a mess and all the drawers were hanging out. When Dad intimated that she might want to try using a mop and soap, Mom said it was already perfect. And she pretended to talk on the phone with her realtor who had just found the ideal house for her—a five bedroom ranch house on a five acre lot. And with enough space for an outdoor pig pen, of course.

I wasn't sure how long she could keep this up. It was strange seeing Mom talking to herself on the phone with an imaginary broker. And Dad was just laughing his head off. *"Hahahahaha!* Who are you talking to? Your imaginary friend?"

"Shush! It's my realtor, Shelly. Don't be rude, honey. She found the perfect house for us. We're in the process of negotiations."

"Hahahahaha! Why don't you imagine a jet and fly over there! *Cackakakakakakaaaaa!"* Dad ran off with his arms flailing. "I'm a *cuckoo!* I'm a *cuckoo!"*

Mom remained undaunted. She was on chapter seven now and was determined to prove him wrong. One of the important things about the Law of Attraction was faith, the book said. You had to have unwavering faith and confidence. Faith served as a pillar for the Law of Attraction and the fecund ground from which hopes manifest. But doubt is the crack and poison in the soil. The ground becomes barren, infertile, and ugly. Unattractive. It's like a woman with bad breath and a man without money.

I admired her stoic discipline. She sat in front of the vision board on a giant cushion, legs crossed, and quietly meditated. She stared at each one of her dreams and aspirations with deep longing. But her demeanor seemed to oscillate between hope and despair. The corners of her piggy lips pointed up, then down, then up again like undulating ocean waves.

* * *

My science teacher, Mrs. Porter, says that in quantum mechanics there's something called the *observer effect.* In the world of the very small, there are phenomenon that cannot be explained by classical physics. For instance, traditional physics can describe the behavior of tables and chairs, but not subatomic particles like electrons. In order to reconcile these conflicting observations, the science of quantum mechanics arose.

"Quantum mechanics, also known as quantum theory and quantum physics, teaches that at the atomic and subatomic scale, simply observing a phenomenon changes that phenomenon," she explained. Mrs. Porter was a brainy teacher that graduated from CalMech and MIZ with honors. Her father helped land astronauts on the moon. I assume she knows what she's talking about. "Things do not appear to exist independently but as the result of an *observer*. The very act of *watching* permanently shapes the nature of reality. Physicists call it the *observer effect*. The implications may be profound."

More astounding, many physicists believe that the entire universe may be a series of probabilities that only become *real* when someone or something observes it into existence.

It seemed to be a lot *woo woo* stuff that borders on the supernatural. But Mrs. Porter said we should be careful about scientism and pseudoscience. She said people often use scientific language and research to support all kinds of crackpot ideas that the underlying data doesn't actually support. Science is a useful tool, she cautioned, but it operates within specific boundaries. It makes assumptions about what is *real* and not, which may or may not be true in a wider philosophical sense. It can be a mistake to apply science outside its provincial borders.

Is the Law of Attraction pure *woo woo* or the yellow brick road to *woo hoo*? Science or phooey pseudoscience? I'm not sure, but the Law of Attraction contends that like the *observer* in quantum mechanics, our thoughts shape the fabric of the physical world. Every moment contains the seeds of multiple latent realities. What appears is not a foregone conclusion, but arises as a result of our thinking minds. We create the reality we observe every moment.

For a kid, it's an appealing idea. But kids also know that what we think often don't happen. Kids imagine things all the time but few of it ever occurs. Yesterday, I thought it was Friday. All day I walked around thinking it was Friday. But it turned out to be Thursday. *Bummer.*

Today, I think it's Friday, and it is. Does that mean I brought Friday into reality because of my thoughts? Or was Friday going to happen whether I believed it or not? I asked my history teacher.

"You're getting into deep waters, Sam," Mr. Johnson said, twisting and tugging at the end of his long mustache. "It's a very complex subject and not without controversy. There are branches of philosophy that study these topics like the philosophy of mind, realism, idealism, and consciousness. Many religions attempt to tackle this subject as well. It's not easy to understand."

"But is it true?" I demanded to know. "Can we create reality with our minds? By just thinking it?"

"It's not that simple. According to some philosophers, in a way you can. But not in the way you think you can."

"What? What do you mean? I'm confused."

"Hahahaha! I know. Let's just say that you can't make a million dollars appear by just thinking it. Or at least that's never worked for me. But in a way, you can if you work at it."

"Oh, the law of work!" I said. "Mr. McCoy said the world is governed by the law of math and work. One plus one is always equal to two."

"*Hahahaha!* Yes, but it's not just working in isolation. Thinking and action can't be disconnected. They're like two faces of a coin. Right actions are often tethered to right thoughts. Pessimists never get anything done. The best thoughts are married to action, not divorced from it. And actions without correct thoughts can be disastrous."

My vegan teacher, Ms. Jones, was a big fan of positive thinking and healthy living, but she wasn't quite convinced just *thinking* was enough. She had to work very hard to obtain her rock hard yoga body.

"I think I understand what you're saying, Sam. But I don't know if there's a strong correlation between the subatomic level and the conventional world," she said. "The ground, for instance, is hard and stays hard whether I observe it or not. But even assuming there's a causal relationship, who exactly is the *observer?* Is it just *me* or all of *us?*"

"Ummm . . . I guess you're observing. And I'm observing. We're both observing," I said.

"Sure, but are we two independent observers? Or the same one observer that only appears to be independent? We're not mental islands. We should avoid the trap of *solipsism.*"

Solipsism was another branch of arcane philosophy. It's the view that only our subjective minds are real. The world itself is a reflection of that subjective mind. And nothing is real outside our own minds. Your world exists in your mind. My world exists in my mind. And the bird's world exists in the bird's mind. Like a dream, everything in the world exists in the mind of the dreamer. *But who is the ultimate dreamer?*

* * *

Mom was coming to her wits end. She kept talking to her imaginary broker on the phone, but no house materialized. She walked around the living room in her bathing suit, but no bikini body appeared. Mom imagined a new minivan in the driveway, but Dad refused to buy a new car.

She meditated in front of her alter of dreams, affirming each of her pinned photos and words on the board one by one like *mantras*. But so far, the universe was not moving for her. What was appearing was the same thing that had appeared in the past. No new reality. Quantum theory was a dud. The wave function was collapsing into smoky air. Mom, the observer, was seeing the same old movie. Same props. Same stage. Same storyline.

She sat in the living room, depressed. An empire of pessimism expanded through her mental terrain. Barbarian hordes from all four directions lay siege to her citadel of hopes and dreams. She didn't want to do anything. She had no motivation. Not even food could extract her from the sofa. Her mud bath was no longer a siren song but symbolized black pools of shattered expectations.

"Come on, honey. I was only joking. Cheer up!" Dad was sorry he made fun of her. "Should I order some pizza? You don't have to cook tonight. Pizza and soda pop for everyone."

"No . . . I wasn't even thinking pizza. I was thinking chicken. I can't even get chicken!"

"Chicken? No problem! I'll go get some chicken. Just think it, and it'll be my command. I'm your genie."

"You're being sweet. If only you were always this way . . ."

"Well, I can't be the dreamboat in your vision board! I'm not the young dashing warthog I used to be, you know. Cut me some slack! *Wahhhooooo! HAAAAAAAAAAAA!*"

"There you go again. Yelling." She was dejected.

"I wasn't yelling! I just have a loud voice. I've always had a loud voice. Even when I was a kid. You know that!"

"Yeah, but it was somehow charming when you were just nine. A little warthog with freckles."

"I'm the same old little warthog you met when we were in grammar school. Nothing's changed but dates on the calendar and a few gray hairs. You really want that new minivan? I guess we can sell the old one."

"No. We shouldn't waste money on a new car. The old one works perfectly fine. I was hoping a new car would just fall from the sky."

"Now, don't be silly, honey. Cars don't fall from the sky."

"I know now. Neither do dreams . . ."

* * *

Danny and Scott came by after school and we went to the park to ride our skateboards. We jumped down steps, slid on rails, and jumped off makeshift ramps we made. Danny tried to grind off the park table and almost split his head open. None of us were wearing helmets. The park was a potential insurance disaster.

"Wow, man. You almost died!" said Scott. "You're lucky

you didn't crack your head! Just a few inches and you could have hit that big rock."

"I think I busted my tailbone. Ouch!" Danny cried.

He was supine on the grass. No blood. The injury was internal. The three of us lied on the ground and stared at the cloud filled sky.

"Maybe we can control the clouds if we all concentrated together," Danny said.

"Hahaha! Okay, let's try," said Scott.

No use. The clouds seemed to just go their own way.

Are luck and randomness underrated? If Danny was just a little less careful or unlucky, he could have hurt more than his butt. He could be in the emergency room. Chance and randomness seemed to be all around us. Not only did we have limited control over the world, it often seemed arbitrary and capricious. Maybe it wasn't just our thoughts and actions that determined fate, but luck too? Unfortunately, by its very nature, luck was something none of us can control. It comes and goes like cumulus clouds.

*   *   *

It appeared Mom had thrown in the towel. Battle fatigue had settled in. Whatever she was doing wasn't working. It was hard to sustain the illusion of victory in the trail of endless defeat. She needed a little emotional peppering up. The physical terrain we can cede, but not the territory of our minds.

We went to the local mall to stretch our legs, amuse our eyes, and arouse Mom's serotonin. I also needed new underwear. Food wasn't working, maybe a little Guffi, Fendu, and Payfewer Shoes will brighten her mood. Mom was usually happy and effervescent. Food made her ebullient. But when the Law of Attraction promised her the universe and she got nothing, the glass half full started to look like a glass nearing empty. Maybe I could help her to see that she had a really gigantic sized cup?

"So many shoppers!" Mom complained. "They tell us retail is going out of business. Restaurants are going out of business. But the crowds always seem so big. Where do they get all the money?"

It was Saturday, 11 a.m. And the mall was packed. It was crowded at the restaurants, department stores, boutique shops, and all the benches. There wasn't a single place to sit to rest our legs from all that stretching. Mom's feet were hurting so much she wanted to regress to walking on fours and jump into the fountain. Luckily, I spotted an open seat on a bench next to a coffee shop and forestalled an embarrassing moment. I ran and saved a spot for Mom.

"Thanks, honey. You're a darling. Here's ten dollars. Go get a Frappurrino or whatever they call it. But decaf for you. An extra large for me. Triple shot of espresso."

Commerce can be an interesting thing for a kid to observe. The hullabaloo. Noise. The change of money for stuff. And if that stuff is food, it soon just disappears. It's like your money just disappeared. But the money you gave in exchange for that stuff is still there. One half of the transaction vanished. But the money didn't. What's going on?

Did we get gypped? Around and around money goes, buying stuff. Some of that stuff is stored in people's houses. Or it disappears into people's stomachs. Or it entertains people for a while and then it gets tossed into the trash. Strange.

Money itself is almost intrinsically worthless too. It's usually a small, smelly piece of paper. Or a metallic coin. Or digital information stored on chips and magnetic stripes on plastic cards. If I didn't know better, someone is probably printing money out of some old bank building somewhere in Washington like the Wizard of Oz with a fancy title like *Chairman*.

I brought Mom her extra large Frappurrino with a triple shot of espresso. The girl behind the counter with tribal tattoos on her neck asked whether it was for me. She said I'd better be careful or else I could overdose.

"What happens if I overdose?" I asked.

"I'm not sure. You'll probably run around like a crazy kid and scream your nose off," she answered. Sounds like Dad. "And your heartbeat will rise dangerously high. Like a million beats per nanosecond."

A lot of people seem to have tattoos these days. Maybe we're all devolving to a more primitive state. The pull of atavism seems to be strong. The rich are getting richer and the poor are turning to self-flagellation. Soon, everyone will have bone piercings through their nose like tribesmen. We'll live on dirt floors under canopies. The poor have to pay penance for their sins.

Pete, who went to San Francisco for a music recital, said he saw lots of people living in tents and pooping on the street. It smelled everywhere. San Francisco used to be a nice town. I wonder if it has anything to do with the Chairman?

When Mom felt a little chipper, we gave up our seats to three tired old ladies and went into the department store to find my underwear. So many kinds of underwear. Briefs. Boxers. Boxer briefs. Boxer trunks. Mom was confused. I was confused. She wished Dad was here. But Dad stopped wearing underwear years ago.

"I remember when all there was were briefs and boxers," Mom said. "It's so confusing now."

"Maybe I'll just try them all and see which ones I like."

"Okay, honey. Take one of each here. I hope it's okay to rip these open . . ."

I slipped into the change room and examined the underwear. One had a little pocket. The boxer briefs and boxer trunks seemed to be similar, except the boxer briefs were a little longer in the legs. And of course, the briefs were just plain traditional briefs. And boxers were plain traditional boxers.

"You alright in there, Sam? You want me to take a look?"

"No, Mom! I'm fine. I think I've decided." The last thing a boy wants is for his mom to *take a look.* I mean, come on!

I was familiar with briefs and boxers. So I decided to try the boxer trunks, which seemed to be a compromise between plain briefs and boxer briefs. I didn't know shopping for underwear could be so confusing!

Mom's stomach was rumbling again, and she wanted a snack before heading home. We ambled over to the food court and ordered some Chinese food. Mom's a big fan of Chinese food. But who isn't?

Mom got a jumbo size soda but she was already half way

through. "Mom, is your soda half full or half empty?" I asked.

"Well. I don't know. Half empty. Wait, half full . . ."

"It's all *perspective*, isn't it, Mom?"

"That's what I said! It's just perspective."

"But perspective is also not enough. We came to the mall because we couldn't just imagine underwear into existence. We had to get in our car, drive half an hour, try out some underwear, and then buy it."

"Well, you tried out the underwear. And I bought them. I asked to take a look but you wouldn't let me."

"The point is, Mom, thoughts are important, but we can't just think and hope for underwear to drop from the sky. Our thinking and acting have to work together like two sides of a coin. We're not mental islands. We shouldn't conflate science with pseudoscience."

"That's true. Cars and underwear don't fall from the sky. At least not yet."

"My teacher calls it *solipsism*."

"Solip—what?"

No surprise, it was hard to understand. It was hard for me to understand. But I tried to explain that we probably can't just imagine things into existence. The physical and mental worlds are designed to coexist. They're neither separate nor wholly the same, but embrace each other like interlocking fingers. Benign thoughts should cohere to benign actions. Congruence is crucial. And a little luck doesn't hurt either.

* * *

The trip to the mall and Chinese food seemed to boost Mom's *happy chemicals*. Like good Bolivian soldiers, they were marching left and right in perfect unison. Per the orders of *el capitan*, the corners of her lips began to point up more often than it pointed down.

After dinner, Mom took repose in her mud bath and told herself that she was happy just as she was right now. A pinned quote on her vision board read, *"Happiness doesn't depend upon who you are or what you have; it depends solely upon what you think."* She tried not to think about the raucous outside. Dad was watching a baseball game and screaming every five minutes.

6:56. *"Yeah!"*

7:01. *"Yeah!"*

7:06. *"Yeah!"*

7:11. *"No!"*

7:16. *"NOOO! @#$%^&!"*

7:21. *"S@%t! WHAT THE @#$%^&?!"*

Mom wanted to believe that she didn't need diamonds, pearls, and quiet to be happy, but how can you want something and be perfectly happy at the same time? The question seemed to be a thorny paradox. Was it a riddle without answer?

Ms. Jones used the example of an apple seed to explain. An apple seed is perfect just as it is. But notwithstanding its perfection, it will grow into an apple tree. And there is no point between being an apple seed and giant apple tree that it stops being perfect, just as it is. From a biological standpoint, there is no stage in its life cycle that it is *imperfect*. Everything, in some way, is just like that, Ms. Jones said.

"Mom, don't you want me to grow up and be a man?" I asked. "Go to college, graduate, and get a good job? Fall in love, get married, and have lots of piglets?"

"Yes, of course. I want all those things for you!" Mom answered.

"But at the same time, aren't you happy with what I am right now? A twelve-year-old, snotty, little boy?"

"Of course, Sam. I wish you'd never grow up! I want you to stay a snotty boy as long as you can."

I didn't want to stay a little kid forever, but I think Mom began to get the picture. The paradox seemed a little less mysterious. And the mystery was beginning to give up its secrets. Mom's floppy ears started to flap as if gears were turning inside her head. If we can accept the present moment like a seed still evolving, then it makes sense that we can love things for what it is now and for what it will also be in the *fullness of time.*

* * *

Mom continued to meditate in front of her vision board, but with a different sort of outlook. She wasn't meditating in lack but her glass full. She was content with her body. She was happy with her house. She was grateful for Dad. Her vision board didn't represent a goal she had to achieve but served as a direction for her to go. It represented a journey of growth and maturation that is never ending.

"Are you still doing that vision board?" Dad asked. "I think I might make a vision board too."

"That's a great idea, honey. What do you want to put on it?"

"Oh, pictures of big, juicy steak. Giant bass. Jumbo sized lobster. Bigger tusks. I've always wanted bigger tusks."

"Your tusks are fine. They're the perfect size for a warthog."

"Thanks, honey. I knew I was perfect! *Wahhooooo!*" Dad howled and ran off.

Dad could be a boor, but there was a softer side to him as well. This morning he found the biggest watermelons and sweet potatoes he had ever seen for sale by organic farmers on the side of the road. It was super expensive, but he bought them for Mom and she was very happy. He said it fell from the sky just as she hoped. Mom knew it came from his heart, which was probably better.

Mr. Johnson says reality is a mixture of the predictable and unpredictable. We can't choose where we start off in life. We can only try to shape what happens after. Grousing doesn't help. It just makes us angry and bitter and that can be poison. But wherever we are, in whatever situation, we can work to improve it at least a little bit. Repeat *that* and we could be getting somewhere.

Maybe we have to deal with the cards as they appear. Like a play, we all have our parts on the universal stage, individually, or perhaps together. Like characters in a dream, we only appear to be separate. The lines aren't fixed. There are opportunities to bend the plot through ad-lib and will. But no single person can rewrite the story. Worldbuilding isn't the solo project of a single, lonely author but the crowd effort of connected minds.

Mom also tried to connect her actions with her thoughts as well. Being two sides of the same coin, she began to see that thoughts alone can't do it all nor actions by themselves divorced from thoughts.

She had fewer feedings between meals to work toward a reasonable weight that was realistic for her. She began to put a little extra money away for nice things like Brada handbags and organic melons. And she tried to be grateful for all the things she already had knowing that everything was also *perfect* in its own way.

Half full or half empty? The measuring stick gives the same reading. But perhaps life isn't measured by rulers but the *qualia* of our minds. There's something to our thoughts. Maybe they do multiply outside our heads in some mysterious way. But for sure they multiply inside. And when it's shared it can spread like viral memes. It's nice to think that we can loll in our mud baths and shape the world with thoughts full of wishes. But it's probably the collaboration of the subjective and objective, the inside and outside, that draws the full picture of our lives.

12

THE BICYCLE RIDE

*"She hops on the rear bike rack and signals for
me to go. 'Giddy-up!' What am I, a horse?"*

SATURDAY 11:51 A.M.

When I get to the school committee meeting, it's
over an hour late. The other members, Billy and
Judy, are making plans and chatting with
carnival organizers. Judy is the class treasurer. Billy is
slumming to help his mom between college courses and
Arabic lessons. His mom, Mrs. Chao, made mooncakes. I
wish I could have mooncakes.

But then I notice Ms. Fearstein, my English teacher.
What is she doing *here?* She's not supposed to be *here!* She's
not a member of the committee. I wouldn't have come if I

knew she was going to be *here!*

"Terrible! Terrible!" she scolds. "You're over an hour late. Almost two hours."

Does she ever have anything nice to say?

"Sorry, Ms. Fearstein. I rode my bike . . . and then there was an accident. Actually, a couple accidents. And a goat . . ."

She sees my mouth moving but isn't paying attention to the words. To her it's just noise like crickets demanding attention.

"And where's Martha? Her father called hours ago and said you were giving her a ride."

"Her Mom was in an acci—" I'm interrupted by a text message Ms. Fearstein receives from Martha's mother, Mrs. Sukova.

"Never mind. She's at the hospital. Probably you're doing, no doubt! Why are you such a horrible boy!"

"No! No!—" I desperately try to plead.

Mrs. Chao recognizes me and waves hello. She offers me mooncakes. I wish I was on another planet.

"And your mother came by with cookies half an hour ago. Where did she learn to bake, anyway?" Ms. Fearstein growls. "At a stable? They're just awful! Awful! Just like you!"

Oh, boy . . .

SATURDAY 11:23 A.M.

It begins to dawn on us that if Martha had been sitting in the front seat, she would have been seriously hurt. Maybe kaput.

"If Sam hadn't given you a ride, I don't want to imagine what could have happened to you!" Mrs. Sukova says, sounding pretty shaken.

We look over at the car. The passenger side is torn up and mangled. Anyone sitting there would have a lot more than a concussion or bloody knee. Shivers run up Martha's spine. She was feeling fortunate to have a spine.

"I might be dead . . ." Martha mumbles.

"Your knee!" cries Mrs. Sukova. "You were in an accident?"

"Oh, I'm okay, Mom. Just a little scratch," says Martha. "Sam fixed me up. He was my doctor today."

"We crashed into some bushes," I confess.

"I was tickling him," Martha says.

SATURDAY 11:18 A.M.

She stumbles out of the car holding her head.

"Mom, Mom!" Martha screams. The tall, wobbly woman is her mother. The crushed, white sedan is her family car.

"Martha, what are you doing here?" her Mom asks. "What happened to you? Who in the world did your makeup?"

"Oh, we were just playing in the drugstore. Your hair! Cupcakes!"

"Are you okay, Mrs. Sukova?" I interrupt.

"I think so . . ." She looks physically okay but probably in shock. "I saw an animal. And then I swerved. And then the truck ran into me . . . Oh, the cupcakes! All wasted . . ."

"You'd better sit down, mam," a police officer says, helping her to a bench. "An ambulance is on its way. You might have a concussion."

SATURDAY 11:16 A.M.

A white sedan is crushed in half in a side collision by a truck. Cupcakes are everywhere like confetti. The poor car looks like it was smashed by a giant boulder from outer space.

People gather around for a better view. The crazy goat seems to have gotten away but the police are on the scene.

A tall woman emerges from the sedan looking dazed and confused. Her top is camouflaged with crumbs and shattered cupcakes hide in her hair like broken soldiers.

SATURDAY 11:14 A.M.

A hoofed animal gallops past us. It's that crazy goat! High BMI police officers are doing their best to apprehend it but they're at least two buildings behind. They're huffing and puffing. They must have been on the chase for blocks.

The goat jumps into the middle of traffic. *KABOOM!* Cars crash. It sounds like a bomb explosion. *MOAB.* The mother of all bombs.

Martha and I run to assess the terrible accident.

SATURDAY 11:04 A.M.

We're sitting on the bus bench with the first aid kit. People walk past staring because her face is painted with exaggerated mascara, lipstick, and eyeliner. It looks like a kid did it. She is still a kid.

I go to work on the bloody knee. I clean her up with some water. Apply disinfectant. *STING!* And then put on the bandage.

"Now you're good as new!" I announce.

"What's wrong with the way I was?" Martha says with a mocking pout.

"Nothing," I think. Except she's a girl, which can be problematic in its own way for a boy.

"Then how can I be as good as new?"

"Because I cleaned up your legs. As for your face, I can't help you with that!"

"What's wrong with my face?"

SATURDAY 10:56 A.M.

Martha is decked up in warpaint. Eyeliner, lipstick, blush, eye shadow, mascara. She seems to be in her element in the makeup aisle.

"Are you going to take scalps?" I ask.

"*Ha! Ha!* Yes, yours!"

"I got you bandages. We have to make you look presentable."

"*Awww . . .* Thanks. You're my hero. My nurse."

"You almost look fifteen with all that on."

"Really? I can't wait till I'm fifteen. Three more years. Then it'll be Paris. Milan. Berlin. Moscow . . ."

Martha sounded older beyond her years. She was just twelve but seemed to know secrets about life boys my age couldn't imagine. We played with lawn darts and rode skateboards. She looked forward to walking down runways in Madrid wearing haute couture and drinking espresso in Parisian cafes.

"What about school? And college?" I ask.

"I'll hire a tutor. And I can go to college after my career is over."

"I can't wait till I'm sixteen. Then I can drive."

"If you drive like you ride your bike, you'll be a dangerous menace on the road! *KABOOM!*"

SATURDAY 10:40 A.M.

We're back in the north part of town near the park, I think. Just a few more blocks my guts tell me. Or is it butterflies?

I see a drugstore and tell Martha that we should get her bandages for the scratch. Blood is dripping down to her ankles. Her leg looks like it was mauled by a squirrel. I don't want her parents to think I'm irresponsible. Hopefully the store has something for under four dollars.

I beeline for the first aid aisle. There's disinfectants. $4. Bandages. $2.50. *Hmmm* . . . I wish I could get disinfectants and bandages. And something to clean up her leg. I turn around to check for Martha, and she's nowhere. She must be in another aisle.

Ahhhh! A mini first aid kit. $3.60. Jeez, do I have enough including sales tax? Darn it! I can't do it in my head. I need to find the electronic aisle.

I grab the calculator and punch in the math. 3.6 X 1.09 = 3.92. Terrific! Eight cents to spare.

Where's Martha?

SATURDAY 10:25 A.M.

"Uh oh! *Ahhhh!*" I shout. *CRASH!* I ride the bike into a crevice and smash into bushes. The giggling and small talk from the passenger side have taken its psychological toll on me. It would on any boy.

"Are you alright?" I ask.

"Yeah, just scratched my knee. *Ouch!*" Martha whimpers. "I should call you *Crash* from now on."

"Let me see." It was a minor scratch. Not too deep. Small bruise. No big deal. I get it all the time. I try to gently pat the dirt away with my hands.

"Thanks, Sam. That's sweet . . ."

"I can't leave you all dirty," I awkwardly say.

"Hahaha!" she crows. "A girl values her safety, you know. And chivalry."

Martha has no brothers, and except for her father, boys were a novelty to her. Her knee starts to bleed.

SATURDAY 10:16 A.M.

We are riding on the dirt road next to the Suidae River. When it rains the river swells up and floods the embankment. When it dries, the sun leaves the ground with deep, sharp crevices everywhere.

"Do you know where you're going?" Martha asks.

"Not exactly," I answer. "But I can navigate through feeling."

"Feels like you ate a lot of cotton candy! *Hahaha!*" she laughs grabbing on tight to my stomach.

"I had a big breakfast," I explain. "Wheaties." Breakfast of champions. I couldn't believe a girl was making me feel self-conscious about my body. Doesn't she know I'm probably the fastest boy in school?

"Didn't you get into a fight with Nathan?" Now she was really probing into my soft spot.

"Yeah . . ."

"I thought that was brave. He's really big. Why were you fighting?"

"I'm not sure. I said something and he just punched me."

"*Hahaha!* You're silly! But you must have gotten him good because I heard him crying in the principal's office."

"Really?" Now I felt bad for Nathan. "Maybe we should switch places so I can check how much cotton candy you had!" I say.

"No, no! I have to be skinny. When I turn fifteen, I'm going to be a model. My mother was a model in the Czech Republic."

Martha was a girl who possessed the easy confidence of a

pretty teenager. Maybe it's inherited. She was a brunette with green eyes and skinny legs. She explains to me that her family is from Eastern Europe where all the famous models come from. Her native soil produces runway models the way we grow ears of corn and stalks of wheat.

For a moment I want to tell her about Cornwall and the time my mom's ancestors were served for dinner at the royal court. Or the time I almost hit the farmer between the eye with my slingshot. But I decide against it.

SATURDAY 10:11 A.M.

"Come on! We'd better go," I say.

We've been watching the street performers for over half an hour. We really have to get going. I'm pretty sure I'm going to get into trouble. Now it's just a question of magnitude. I pull up the bike and Martha hops on the back.

"That was fun!" she says. "I guess they'll be performing at the carnival."

"Yup."

"How much money you think we could make today?"

"Not sure. Last year they raised six hundred dollars."

"I hope there will be time to enjoy the carnival too. Let's go on the buccaneer ride. I promise I won't scream into your ear."

"I don't know—"

"Hey! What's that?" Martha yells. It looks like a goat on the loose. It's butting pedestrians and knocking over display tables on the street.

"Maybe a carnival animal?" I say. "That goat is going to cause a traffic accident and maybe get someone killed. We'd better stay clear."

I take another detour. I wasn't exactly sure about directions. I could be lost.

SATURDAY 9:36 A.M.

Martha is with the pantomime actors trying to copy their moves. There's supposed to be an invisible wall separating them but she keeps poking through like there's nothing there. She's not cohering to the laws of the pantomime world. She's not a very good pantomime actor.

I get on the giant trampoline and try to do back flips. It's soft enough so that I can't really hurt myself. I keep landing on my head and Martha laughs.

A knife thrower asks for volunteers. She offers her body in sacrifice. I tell Martha, "*No!*" It could be dangerous. Somehow, I'm feeling parental. The man asks Martha to step forward because she's the prettiest girl in the crowd. "She's a kid, a minor!" I yell. Everyone boos me.

They blindfold her and tie her up against a weird apparatus. The man pretends to throw knives at her. But actually, knives pop up from behind a screen I'm told. But I swear I see knives flying through the air! What's going on? What diabolical legerdemain is this?

When it's all over, Martha is giddy with excitement. She jumps up and down with both hands on my shoulders. The crowd cheers with applause. She tells me she was *sure* she was going to die.

I want to say I saved her but it wouldn't be true.

SATURDAY 9:21 A.M.

"My mother's baking cupcakes," Martha offers in small talk. She has her arms so tight around my waist I feel like we're almost engaged. "What's your mom baking?"

"She's doing cookies. Chocolate chip. Peanut butter. Marshmallow . . ."

"That sounds yummy!"

"*Bleh!* It's okay for her first try, I guess."

We make our way through Central Ave. and there's a mini performance in the middle of the street. I guess it's some kind of promotion for the carnival.

"Oh, let's stop and watch the street performance!" Martha says.

"But we have to get to—"

"Please! For just a quick second!"

I stop next to the crowd and we watch the performers pretending to crash into invisible walls, defy gravity on trampolines, and breathe fire.

"I wish I could breathe fire!" Martha says.

"Maybe you do . . . in the morning!" I remark. She looks at me and pretends to be angry. Or maybe it's real?

A clown is walking around selling cotton candy. "I love cotton candy," Martha tells me. But what kid doesn't love cotton candy? "Do you have any money?"

"Yeah, I have five bucks," I tell her but instantly regret it.

I think I shouldn't have told her anything.

"Can I borrow a dollar?"

"Ummm . . . okay." I hand her a dollar and she buys two cotton candies for fifty cents a piece. She hands me one.

"Here, I bought one for you too!" she says with a grand gesture of generosity. Except, it was my money!

"Thanks," I mutter. She's going to be a terror when she grows up.

SATURDAY 9:16 A.M.

I'm riding through unfamiliar territory. The trees are greener. The lawns are beautifully groomed. And unbeknownst to me, I'm riding to Martha's house. I didn't know she lived around here. Uh oh, I see that her father is having car trouble. But no flat tire. Something with the starter. It's just *"click, click, click, click, click . . ."*

Martha spots me and runs up. Why is she doing that? She's all legs. I just want to ride past.

"Sam! Sam! Are you going to the carnival?"

"Yeah . . ." I answer with mild trepidation. What does she want?

"Can you give me a ride on the back of your bicycle? Dad's having trouble with the car."

Give her a ride? I'm about to say, *"no way, Jose!"* but her mom comes out and thanks me.

"That's so nice of you, Sam! You're a life saver!" she hollers with a peculiar accent. "Now, Martha, be careful to hold on tight. I'll be over with the cupcakes in about an hour."

I was afraid of that. She hops on the rear bike rack and signals for me to go. *"Giddy-up!"*

What am I, a horse?

SATURDAY 9:02 A.M.

Dad's sniffing around the front yard and notices holes everywhere.

"Were you playing with lawn darts, Sam?! I told you not to play with that in the front yard!"

"Sorry, Dad. The guys were over and threw it around," I explain.

Suddenly he notices the flat tire and realizes it was caused by one of the darts. He starts to fume.

"Arrggghhh! Gaddarnit! Sammmm! You and your friends blew out a tire!"

I quickly grab my bicycle to avoid the coming storm and imminent fracas.

"Dad, I'm gonna ride my bike over to the carnival!" I yell. "Sorry about the tire! Forgot to tell you!" I dash away in a hurry.

Whew! That was close. His temper tantrum could go on for hours.

I avoid the main road and wind my way through obscure residential streets to throw Dad off the trail. I don't want to be surprised by a wild boar on the chase. He's been known to do that, you know. It scares the bejesus out of me.

SATURDAY 8:47 A.M.

The kitchen table is edge to edge with Mom's freshly baked cookies. Raisin cookies. Peanut butter cookies. Marshmallow cookies. Oatmeal cookies. Chocolate chip cookies. Sweet potato cookies. Candy cookies. I'm not sure where she came up with these recipes. I didn't know Mom could bake cookies. I think she's just winging it. Something seems *off*.

"Wow, lots of cookies, Mom!" I say.

"I've been baking since early this morning. Hard to believe, eh?"

"When did you learn to bake cookies?"

"This morning. I'm just winging it."

I take a cookie to have a taste. *Bleh!* Yuck.

"How is it?" she asks.

"Pretty good . . ."

SATURDAY 8:28 A.M.

Today is bake sale day at the carnival on the other side of town. The school is holding its annual money drive. I'm a member of the planning committee with Billy, Martha, and Judy. All the parents who volunteered are making cookies, pies, and other stuff to sell. The planning committee is supposed to arrive a couple hours early to discuss something —I have no clue what. Dad's going to drive me, but he's still snoozing away.

"Dad! Get up!" I yell. He's sleeping like a two ton, moss

covered log.

"*Arururur* . . . can't you ride your bike or something?" he grumbles.

"It's far, on the other side of town, Dad! Come on, get up. I can't be late!"

"*Arururur* . . . oh jeez! . . . waking me up early on a Saturday!" he whines. He lumbers out of bed and coughs up phlegm into the sink. "*Archhhuuuchucucuchh!*"

I run out to avoid having to witness the morning din. The awful cacophony is too much for a sensitive boy to bear.

FRIDAY 7:06 P.M.

The guys and I are out throwing lawn darts in the front yard. The lawn isn't very big so we try to see who could hit the mark the closest from three houses down.

Scott throws it up in the air and it comes crashing down on a neighbor's roof. Danny almost spears a poodle. The owner gives us the evil eye and tells us we'd better stop throwing darts into the air.

A few of our darts go into the backyard of neighbors on the other side of the street. We hope we didn't kill anyone.

I toss one like a football and it hits Dad's minivan in the tire. *Pop!* The air is coming out. It'll be flat by tomorrow morning. Dad's sure gonna be mad about this. He's going to scream his head off when he finds out. But at least I didn't break a window. Gotta stay *positive.*

We decide to go to the park and ride our skateboards. There was supposed to be a new ramp some of the kids set up.

It's getting dark and hard to see anything but Danny wants to take the lawn darts anyway. He's gonna throw it up in the air and see where it lands. Scott says we could tape mini LED lights to it. That would be stupid sick! He has a bunch of them at home.

I think tomorrow is going to be a good day. The school is selling cupcakes and cookies at the carnival. I'm going to secretly stuff myself and sneak into all the rides.

13

BAD HAIR DAY

*"Why won't they believe me? I'm
just having a bad hair day."*

I don't know how it happened. In hindsight, it's hard to say why I did it. It seemed so easy at the time. I really wanted to do it. It felt urgent. What could possibly go wrong? There were guards to protect me. Danny said it was simple. He did it all the time. Bzzzzz, bzzzzz! All done. Straightforward as stuffing your face with Chocolate Chip Cookie Dough ice cream. No one gets hurt with ice cream!

Scott warned me. He said you can't do it yourself unless you had eyes behind your head and arms growing out your back. He said there's a reason why people hire professionals. Don't be a cheapskate.

But ruefully, I did it anyway. I took the clippers and stood in front of the mirror. And that's when it all went wrong. I gave myself a Kim Jong Un haircut. I looked like the dictator of North Korea except without a kingdom. A sinking feeling dropped into the pit of my stomach when I realized what had happened. I almost collapsed from vertigo. I felt confused, alone, stupefied. And miserable. I have school tomorrow.

I guess I could try to explain the mechanics. Initially it appeared to be going well. The clipper did what it was supposed to do. The guard made sure the miniature lawn mower didn't make contact with skin. I used a number eight guard. I mowed. Mowed. Then somehow, I started to chop. Chop. Don't ask me why. I think I wanted to make sure I got every stalk of hair. Then the guard fell off. And I was still going chop, chop. And I mowed my hair off to the skin. There were several big gashes on the side and back. No way to salvage it. I tried. I really did. It was a choice between cutting everything off, which I don't want to do. And the Kim Jong Un haircut. I didn't know there was a name for it.

* * *

"Hahaha!" Mom unkindly cackled. "I wish your dad was here to see this!"

Dad was away at a plumbing convention in Los Angeles. He'd be back in a couple days. I could have asked Mom to cut my hair, but she has piggly hands. She can't cut boy's hair. She once tried when I was four and gave me an upside down bowl cut. I'm glad I don't remember. Maybe it's repressed. I think it's all coming back to me now.

"Mom! What do I do! It looks horrible!" I cried.

"Stop fussing," she said. "Hair grows back. Someday."

How fast does hair grow? It's times like these that one becomes interested in trivia. According to Mikipedia, human hair grows about half an inch per month. That's approximately .0167 inches a day. It was hopeless!

I texted Danny to ask for advice. He said you're not supposed to whack yourself with clippers. You have to mow gently. How was I supposed to know? I don't do landscaping! I blamed him anyway. I sent him pictures on Instabram and he said my head resembled a giant mushroom. Danny said he uses a number three guard and gives himself a buzz cut. Bzzzzz! Bzzzzz! He could do it with his eyes closed.

Scott shed few tears for me too. I sent him pictures on Facebark, and he gloated, "I told you so!" He's right, he did. But somehow, the pictures went public and now everyone knew. I think my privacy setting was sabotaged by Mark Zukernerd. He's a menace to children. Now I was being electronically crucified by all my classmates. My social media notifications were ringing nonstop. Everyone was tagging me. #KimJongUn #NorthKorea #LittleRocketMan. Where's my safe space? I don't deserve cyber-bullying! Please help me, #FirstLady #Helania!

*   *   *

Embarrassment is a curious thing. Where does it come from, and why does it exist? What does it serve to be timid when confidence gets more points? Or as social animals, does embarrassment serve as a way to force compliance and cooperation from members? Is it a way to twist arms without actual force?

But I want to cooperate! I really do. Just give me back my hair, please! I don't want to be bald or have a mushroom head. I want to fit in like homogenous bees in a hive. Why can't it see that I'm trying my best to be normal? But I'm being punished for something I can't control. Cruel Nature.

I prayed to the gods and asked for a second chance. I closed my eyes and clasped my hands. Turn back time and let me do it all over. I won't mess it up again. I promise! But without oblations, my pleas were ignored. Rapacious gods! I stood in the bathroom in horror, staring at myself. But who was he? That guy!

With trembling and trepidation, I went to school with a giant hat. It covered my entire bald head with a mushroom on top. But when class started, I was asked to remove it. Blood drained out of my brain.

I think I was having an out of body experience. It wasn't me sitting in class but Kim Jong Un. He removed his hat and an explosion of laughter erupted. Someone was testing nukes. Hovering above the classroom, I felt sorry for Kim Jong Un. He doesn't deserve that. He only wants peace.

"Settle down, people!" my math teacher, Mr. McCoy, said. "It's just hair. It'll grow back." Do you promise? When?

"You look funnier in person!" some kid yelled. More combustion of guffaw. Another explosion. Maybe it hit

Guam?

My body was floating higher and higher. I was flying above the school and looking down at a speck of hair. The classroom was so tiny. The traffic of children resembled marching ants. I was fading into the sky. My head was feeling cold. I think I was being sucked into a black hole.

* * *

Somewhere between second and third period, someone stole my hat. I don't know who did it or how, but by now, I was too numb to care. Sensation had left my skin. You could stick a pin in me and I wouldn't feel it. I could be a human voodoo doll. Whatever it is I looked like, I would have to own it. Besides, I'm not my hair. Right?

When I walked into English class, Ms. Fearstein turned ghost white and her knees nearly buckled. "You look like Kim Jong Un!" she screamed. "Get out of my class! Now!"

"I'm not Kim Jong Un!" I protested. "I just look like him! My mom says everyone has bad hair days."

"You're having more than a bad hair day, kiddo!"

"It's just hair. It'll grow back."

"My hair never grew back!" Ms. Fearstein bitterly hissed. She wears a wig.

"You can't judge people by their hair," Laura entreated in my defense. "That's discrimination."

"I judge people by everything!" Ms. Fearstein snarled. "He looks like a little Mussolini from head to toe. My parents fled communist Russia. I don't want a communist sympathizer in my classroom!"

"No, no! Don't be fooled by the hair. I'm not my hair. I'm not a communist sympathizer!" I said. "I don't even know what communism is!"

"Communism is YOU. You are communism!" she accused. "You should be sent to the gulags!"

* * *

After class, I slipped out as fast as I could and tried to lose myself in the anonymity of the crowd. But all cameras were glued on me. I was a walking reality TV show. I was being streamed live on the internet and half the town of Suidae Valley seemed to be watching. We've never had a celebrity in town before.

At lunch, kids came around and asked if I was really Kim Jong Un. I was eating a hamburger and people were intrigued. Apparently, no one's ever seen the leader of North Korea eat a hamburger. I went for a burrito and some kids shrieked. Scott told them to buzz off or I'd nuke them. Danny said Kim Jong Un will execute brats with anti-aircraft missiles. And anyone who continues to annoy the *Marshal* would be killed along with their families. I asked them to stop live streaming and hash tagging me on social media. I wanted my privacy. But they took pictures and tagged me anyway. #KimJongUn #hamburgers #burrito #scary. It's not easy being infamous with a bad haircut.

Koreaboos asked if I was from Korea. I didn't know there was such a thing as Koreaboos. They loved K-Pop and Korean *idol groups* like Big Boom, EXU, BTX, and Bad Pink. I was intrigued that I might possibly resemble these people. They showed me videos on WeTube. It received billions of views. It was breaking records every day. It was like *Gangnam Style,* but better. Why hadn't anyone told me? They were well-dressed, synchronized, and flamboyant. They danced like Michael Jackson, sang like the Beatles, and looked like better looking relatives of Kim Jong Un.

"Are you from South Korea or North Korea," a bleach blonde with blue circle lenses asked. The iris of her eyes were ginormous.

"Ummm . . . actually, I'm neither."

"But you look like Kim Jong Un. You must be from one of the Koreas," another girl said whose eyes resembled green billiard balls. They were all over-dressed for school and seemed to have perfect, flawless skin. *How?*

"Yeah, maybe. I'm not sure. I don't know much about my family history." I was so desperate for acceptance I stretched the truth. I didn't know anything about my family's genealogy, but I doubt it came by way of East Asia.

"Ask your parents. We could be friends if there's any Asian in you," the bleach blonde with jumbo sized eyes propositioned, floating off with her friends, and leaving behind the scent of sweet Asian pears.

I was taking in a long, slow whiff when I noticed the hubbub near the entrance of the school. It seems local reporters wanted a word with me. All the live streaming and social media tagging had reached the press.

"Are you Kim Jong Un?" a reporter from the Suidae Valley Times asked, sticking a mic in my face.

"No, no! I'm not!" I said. "I'm just having a bad hair day!"

"Is this in protest to President Drump's *Fire and Fury*?" a reporter with the Suidae Gazette asked.

"Fire and fury? I have no clue about that. I'm too young to die!"

"Are you a North Korean sympathizer?" asked a journalist from the Bacon Daily News.

"What?! I don't want war. I think peace is good. Can't we all just get along?"

Luckily, the press meeting was interrupted by the school principal who told the reporters to leave. He said I was too young to be interviewed, and they weren't allowed on school grounds. But by tomorrow, my hair would be splashed all over the local papers.

The tabloids suggested that I was Kim Jong Un's long lost son. "KIM JONG UN'S SECRET SON HIDING IN SUIDAE VALLEY." Another paper said I was protesting American foreign policy in Asia. "KID MOCKS U.S. POLICY IN KOREA." Another reported that I was Kim Jong Un in disguise as a little boy. "KIM JONG UN HERE IN SUIDAE VALLEY!"

But why won't they believe me? I'm just having a bad hair day.

* * *

I had to find out what North Korea was about. Who is this Kim Jong Un? Why did he have a funny haircut? Why do people hate him and his country? Why was K-Pop getting billions of views? And why do Koreaboos smell like delicious fruit?

According to Mr. Johnson, my history teacher, North Korea emerged out of the division of the Korean peninsula in the wake of World War II. Two young U.S. officers were assigned to define an American *occupation* zone, and using a National Geographic map, drew a line on the 38th parallel, dividing the peninsula approximately in half. No Koreans were asked. No experts were consulted. A partition was simply imposed. And as a result, two separate and hostile governments emerged. One in the north and the other in the south. He called it a great mistake that would lead to the death of millions and leave a legacy of hostility that continues to this day.

"The history of the Koreas is shrouded in ideological controversy," Mr. Johnson said. "But what we can say without dispute is that the Korean people vehemently protested the partition of their country. But it was this division that planted the seeds for the Korean War in 1950. It was a war for unification, kinda like our Civil War in America, except the secessionists weren't the Korean people themselves."

"Didn't we fight for democracy?" Victoria asked. "South Korea is free. North Korea is a communist prison camp."

"South Korea wasn't always free or democratic," Mr. Johnson said. "Washington installed a police state. And it was a brutal military dictatorship until the late 1980s. America supported every autocratic leader in South Korea from the first to the very last. The South Korean people had to fight for their own democracy. Many died."

"We had to kill the commies!" Steve shouted, his face turning scarlet, matching his eyebrows. "My dad said Russia occupied North Korea and we had to defend South Korea."

"I think your dad is starting in the middle. Remember that the Korean War arose out of the 1945 division," Mr. Johnson explained. "The Korean War is often called the Forgotten War, because no one remembers it, assuming they knew it at all. It was the first proxy war between the U.S. and the USSR in the prelude to the Cold War. Korea's civil war resulted in the death of at least a fifth of the Korean people. United Nations forces, led by the U.S., carpet bombed North Korea. No building was left standing. It was bombed back to the Stone Age. We literally ran out of targets. We used chemical and biological weapons. We committed war crimes. We contemplated nuking North Korea. Over thirty-six thousand American soldiers sacrificed their lives."

"Why do we still hate each other?" I asked. "Why don't we make peace like we did with China and Vietnam? They're communists too."

"Sadly, it's geopolitics," Mr. Johnson answered. "There are twenty-eight thousand American troops stationed in South Korea. We're still technically at war. It remains the last bastion of the Cold War, though that ended in the 1990s. South Korea serves as a military base for America's forward projection into Northeast Asia. North Korea is a useful bogeyman to justify our continued military presence in the region. We say we're there to protect the South from a possible invasion by the North, but in the view of many experts, our real adversary is China and Russia."

"Why do people hate Kim Jong Un? Is he really bad?"

"We don't know much about Kim Jong Un. But mainly, it's our official policy to hate him because he's the leader of North Korea. He represents the regime the same way President Drump represents America. He was born in the wrong place at the wrong time. He inherited a country that, many say, is in America's interest to vilify."

"But why does he have funny hair?"

"I don't think anyone really knows the answer to that, Sam! Maybe he's just having a bad hair day like you!"

It seems some people are just born in the wrong place at the wrong time. And like me, have bad hair days. I hope mine doesn't go on for years and President Drump doesn't pick on me on Twizzer. I'm very sensitive.

*   *   *

In the face of nonstop misunderstanding and teasing, my confidence was drooping like cryptocurrencies. It was making new highs for a while and then this happened. I was being defined by my hair and I was doing just the same. When people saw me, they saw bald sides and a mop top. And like the social rat that I was, I absorbed the prevailing norms and conventions around me. My hair was me. And I was my hair. I started to hate myself for being so weak. Why couldn't I define my own identity?

Mrs. Porter, my science teacher, likened it to synecdoche. Synecdoche is a figure of speech in which a part of something refers to the whole of something. In my case, I was being referred to by my hair and identified with it.

"Of course, you're not a synecdoche," Mrs. Porter explained. She had long silver, white hair that resembled the mane of an old, patrician lion. "A synecdoche is a crude ways to refer to things. But it's more comical and superficial than real. Humans have complex identities."

"Why do people associate me with the dictator of North Korea?" I asked.

"Related to synecdoche is something called metonymy, a figure of speech in which a thing is referred to by another thing closely associated with it. In other words, you're being associated with Kim Jong Un because your hair reminds people of him. But you shouldn't worry too much. Your hair will grow back in a few weeks."

"But that's too long!" I moaned.

"You're not your hair. And the hair isn't you," Mrs. Porter asserted. "And you're not Kim Jong Un, even if you look like him. Rebuff crude caricatures and associations."

But in the real world, pegging people is what we do. We reduce people to their appearance, jobs, and social status. Mr. McCoy said we use rules of thumb and heuristics all the time to make sense of a complex reality. It can be a useful shortcut to solve knotty problems. But it's also a gross oversimplification. While impressions are important, the map isn't the territory. The world isn't flat. No one deserves to be truncated to a two-dimensional cartoon.

How should we define ourselves then? If we're not our hair, our jobs, and diplomas hanging on walls, then what are we? *What am I?*

*   *   *

I was glad to be finally home. After dinner, I laid in bed staring at bumps on the ceiling. Mom thinks I'm making a big ado over nothing. She said it doesn't matter what people say. Your own opinion is what counts. But platitudes are easier said than done. Self-help cliches often prove impotent in the middle of a thunderstorm. My own opinion was like sponge absorbing everything around me. When I looked in the mirror, what looked back wasn't the boy I thought I was yesterday but someone half a world away. It's funny how a small change can shift everything. Humans are so vain.

I asked Laura why she was still nice to me. She said it's because she doesn't care about my hair. She likes me for me. But I had forgotten who I was. What did she see that I didn't?

Danny and Scott didn't make fun of me, either. I guess that's because we're best friends. I was still the same Sam to them. But for everyone else, they only saw hair. I was a silly synecdoche and metonymy. I was a heuristic gone wrong. I was hair, Kim Jong Un, or the ugly cousin of a K-Pop boy band.

Maybe we all need people who don't judge us for our foibles. It reminds us that we're not just that. It makes it easier to not judge ourselves and recognize that there are other qualities that make us what we are or at least aspire to be.

∗ ∗ ∗

The next day, I saw my hair in all the papers. I wanted to run to my room and hide. But I told myself that I'm not the story in the news. I'm not the hair. I refuse to be a synecdoche. I went to school without a hat. And that was a deliberate choice. Besides, someone would probably steal it anyway.

Walking to class, I saw Ms. Jones leaving the teacher's lounge. My health teacher had just gotten back into town. But when she recognized me, it was only smiles. No judgment. No metonymy. I was the same Sam.

"Nice hair, Sam!" Ms. Jones said. "Sorry I missed all the excitement yesterday."

"Just having a bad hair day," I said bashfully.

"No, it's unique. You shouldn't be afraid to experiment. When I was fourteen, I had a mohawk."

"Weren't you teased?"

"Sometimes. But they learned fast that you shouldn't tease girls with mohawks!"

Between third and fourth period, I bumped into Martha. She was clutching today's paper and grinning from high cheekbone to cheekbone.

"Hey, *Crash,* you're famous!" she announced.

"What? Oh! That's nothing."

"That's some groovy hair! You really look like Marshal

Kim of North Korea."

"Yeah, yeah. I've heard the jokes already!"

"No, I mean it in a good way. It's really neat. You stand out. It's so Marxist!"

"Marxist? What do you know about that?"

"My mom's from Eastern Europe, dummy. I grew up hearing about Marxism. She says it's terrible. But I think it's retro cool. So last century."

In English, Ms. Fearstein tried her best to ignore me. But today's papers had gotten around and everyone was talking. Was she jealous of my notoriety? She was unusually civil.

"Wow, I can't believe you're in the papers, Sam," Laura marveled. "You're a celebrity."

"It's just a big misunderstanding."

"Maybe. But you're the most famous person in Suidae Valley. It says here you want world peace?"

"Of course! I don't want war."

"I think that's so cool."

After school, Danny and Scott came over. We did some homework and then went to the park to play basketball. They say that Kim Jong Un loves basketball. Maybe I had more in common with the Marshal than I know? Maybe we all have more in common with each other than we think?

Dad came home and didn't blink an eye when he saw my hair. He didn't seem to notice a thing. I'm not sure whether that's good or not. He just thundered, "I want DIIIINNNNNEEERRR!" And terrorized the neighborhood.

They say knowing yourself is wise but it's probably the opposite of self-consciousness. Whatever we are is only a snapshot in time. Every moment, we're someone different.

I stopped obsessing over my hair. What I am. Or who I was. And maybe that's the way it's supposed to be. When you're playing basketball, just play. When you're doing homework, just study. When you're with your friends, just have fun. When you stop and think about what you are, it's like trying to catch a flowing stream.

THE SWINES

ANECDOTES OF A PIGGLY FAMILY

THE SWINES

About the Author

H.M. So is a Korean-American writer and native of Los Angeles. This is his debut novel.

If you enjoyed this book, please consider a review on Amazon, Goodreads, and other venues. Please share with your family, friends, and on social media.

You can connect with H.M. So on his website at: https://hmso.inkonpages.com.

Or email him directly at: hmso@inkonpages.com

Made in the USA
Coppell, TX
03 July 2021